THE GRA...

Her mind expands until it seems her skull must crack. Then, glowing through the pain like fire through smoke, the words come. She cannot tell whether they are written or spoken; they flicker behind her eyes like hissing neon signs.

'It will be terrible.'

'What will you do?'

'What can you do?'

'Will you try to stop it? We would like that, watching you try to stop it.'

'They will all die.'

She reaches up to block her ears but the words still light up in her head. The creatures gather closer.

She lifts her head and screams . . .

THE GRANITE BEAST

Ann Coburn

RED FOX

For Ticey, whose heart was never empty.

A Red Fox Book

Published by Random Century Children's Books
20 Vauxhall Bridge Road, London SW1V 2SA

A division of the Random Century Group

London Melbourne Sydney Auckland
Johannesburg and agencies throughout the world

First published in 1991 by The Bodley Head Children's Books

Red Fox edition 1992

1 3 5 7 9 10 8 6 4 2

Printed and bound in Great Britain by
Cox & Wyman Ltd, Reading, Berkshire

ISBN 0 09 985970 X

'One day, friend and stranger,
The granite beast will rise
Rubbing the salt sea from his hundred eyes
Sleeping no longer.'

Charles Causley

Chapter One

Ruth was out of bed and running the instant she broke free of the nightmare.

'Get out!' she cried. 'Get out!' And then screamed as her foot thudded into something hard. She crashed to the floor and lay there, winded, spread out like a starfish in the darkness.

I've got to warn them. Something terrible . . . If I could just remember . . .

She held her breath, face fierce with concentration, but the nightmare slipped away.

Shivering with cold, Ruth turned on to her back and sat up slowly, feeling splinters catch at her nightdress. Her skinned toes were throbbing and her right knee was sending out flares of pain with every heartbeat. She was probing it gently, testing the injury, when her spine began to prickle.

This is all wrong.

She moved into a crouch, neck tingling with warning. Her body was ready to run but her mind was still catching up, laboriously spelling out the threat.

Splinters. I'm on a bare floor, a wooden floor. But my bedroom has a carpet. So where . . . ?

Ruth became aware of the darkness. She opened her eyes wide but darkness stood around her, dense and still. She wanted to run but the darkness held her down. Her blind blunderings would make an easy target.

For what?

Ruth bit down a scream. Her neck and back felt so vulnerable, so open to hurt from whatever might be waiting. She listened hard, but solid, soundproof blackness packed the air, rolling and swelling around her like the oily blackness in her dream.

The dream. That's it; I'm still dreaming. Why was I running?

She forced herself to concentrate and fragments of the nightmare began to stir again behind her eyes. Small, blurred figures; a strong, cloying stench . . .

Then the pictures cracked and were gone as a slow, soft chuckle curled from the corner behind her. The air was suddenly heavy with a stink like that of dead fish. Ruth took in a breath that went on and on, filling her lungs until she felt her ribs would crack. Then she screamed.

'Ruth? Ruthie? Are you all right?' Her mother opened the door and hurried in, scattering light from the landing through the room.

'Oh, Mum.'

'Shhh, it's all right now. You had a bad dream, that's all. I heard you yelling.'

'But – where are we?'

'In the new house, remember?'

Ruth felt safe enough to risk a glance round. Bare boards, packing cases, curtainless windows. Nothing lurked in the corners. 'There was something in the room. I heard it – sort of gurgling. And a smell . . .'

'It's an old house, Ruthie. Must've been the plumbing. We'll get it checked.'

'Oh, plumbing,' muttered Ruth, finally back in the real world. Memory returned and the events of the past eight months began to unreel in her head like a bleak silent movie.

Scene one. A middle-aged man lying on the floor, eyes turned blankly to the window and the falling snow. A plump, dark-haired woman is thumping her fists into his chest, making his head jerk violently, but still he stares at the window and the falling snow. The woman covers his mouth with her own, trying to breathe for him, but his stare is unblinking. Cut to the ambulance, wailing flashes of lightning blue through the window. Red blankets and the doctor, shaking his head.

Scene two. Aerial view of a cemetery. Long rows of graves, dirty white piles of snow, and four long, black cars moving towards the grey chapel like slow beetles.

Scene three. A long shot of furniture piled in a sagging heap in the street, shabby in the late-summer sunshine. Cut to a red-haired girl in a bedroom where the shadows of former posters still stand darkly against faded wallpaper.

Scene four. Long shot of a car leaving Coventry and driving south down miles of motorway. Close-up of the girl crouched on the hard shoulder, buffeted by the backwash of speeding lorries, vomit rising in her throat. Pan away to focus on the motorway crows strutting along like black-coated undertakers, waiting for a crash.

Ruth shuddered on the cold floor. Her mother knelt and reached out but she jumped up and turned on the

3

light. 'Why are we doing this, Mum?' Her voice trembled.

'You know why. It's what your dad always wanted. To live in Cornwall, own a shop.'

'But he's not here. He's dead.' Ruth's desperation made her stress each measured word.

'It's what he always wanted,' came the firm, tired repetition.

Ruth glared at the packing cases.

'Do you want to come into my bed?' It sounded more like a plea than an offer, but bitterness surged in Ruth's throat and came out in hurting words.

'No. What I want is for you to go. Now. I'm all right. No need to stay.'

Ruth's mother levered her stout body from the floor and moved to the door. Exhaustion was written in the shadows under her eyes. 'It really is a nice place, love. Wait till you see the view from the front bedroom in the morning. It's a pity we arrived in the dark.' She stopped in the doorway, looking like a plump space monster with curlers spiking out of her head. 'Try to get some sleep. You want to be fresh for your new school in the morning. Goodnight, Ruthie.'

Ruth stared at the floorboards until the door clicked shut, then she walked to the window. Her face looked back from the dark glass. 'You can be a real bitch, Ruth Davis,' she muttered, glaring at her reflection.

From the corner of her eye, Ruth could see her new school uniform set out on the chair. She picked up the grey skirt and jumper and, turning back to the window, held them up against herself for a moment. She stared at the clothes with her own head poking out at the top and wondered what a stranger would think.

4

Leaning closer, she studied each familiar feature as though she was seeing it for the first time. The hair was all right. An unusual pale auburn, like new copper, it was cut in the latest style: short over the ears, tapered at the neck and left long and spiky on top. She had been one of the few girls at school with hair thick enough to carry it off.

Her skin looked white in the harsh glare of an unshaded bulb but it always was pale, even in the best of lights. She never tanned, just collected freckles, mostly on her nose.

Well, they would collect there, she thought. Plenty of room for them. God, what a hook. Ruth winced and widened her eyes to compensate. They were large and oval; a pale, clear green. Envy green her dad had called them, when she used to cry for things she couldn't have. She stared at the window for a moment longer without really seeing, imagining her friends starting their fourth year together, pieces in a familiar pattern.

A shiver brought her back to the cold room. She switched off the light and edged her way to bed, curling down under the quilt for warmth.

Somewhere nearby, another figure sat in the darkness, still shaken by the cry that had smashed through his sleep. The fear had gone now, wherever it had come from, but his face was strained in the glow from a rare cigarette. He understood two things. Something had begun, and someone needed help.

Monday morning brought clear September skies and a slicing wind from the sea. Ruth sneered from the front-bedroom window at the village huddled around a crossroads. One road came down from the moors, running past the house before it dipped to the centre of the village, then crawled up again to a lighthouse perched on the cliff edge. The road which crossed it followed the line of the cliffs in both directions as far as Ruth could see.

Grey stone houses jostled for space at the crossroads, then gradually thinned out into four untidy straggles that followed the roads. Further out, farmhouses grew out of the granite hillsides, crouching low against the weather, and at the edge of the cliffs a row of coastguards' cottages stood next to the lighthouse. Their whitewashed walls were brilliant in the sunshine and the sea sparkled behind them.

Scattered here and there were what looked like very narrow, two-storey houses with strangely tall chimneys spiking the sky. Gaunt and grey, each one stood in isolation, like an unwanted guest at a party, and each one was crumbling and roofless.

Smoke-houses for kippering fish? No, they wouldn't have windows. Ruth turned away, too tired to be curious for long.

'Will you find the way?' asked Mrs Davis as her daughter clattered down the uncarpeted stairs.

'You are joking, aren't you? I could see the school from the front-bedroom window. It's straight down the road to the crossroads and up the other side.'

'Yes, that's right. It's a pretty village, isn't it, with the sea behind it? Did you have a look over the house this morning? And the shop? I know it needs a lot of work, but . . .' Her mother trailed off and peered at Ruth hopefully. There was silence. They both looked at the floor.

'Got to go,' Ruth blurted. 'Mustn't be late.' She

6

turned, almost ran from the house and began the walk to school with her head down and her nerves jumping.

At the crossroads she stopped to survey the main street. On the corner behind her was a dairy and teashop. It had a garden sprouting wobbly tin tables and chairs with rusty legs. Over the road a pub called The King Arthur leaned against a Methodist chapel, which arched its high, cold windows in disdain. There was also a post office, a library and a scattering of small shops. The street was deserted.

'Oh, hell,' muttered Ruth. She had looked ahead in the direction of the school and seen a distant cluster of uniformed figures. Immediately her whole body ached to turn around and head for home. Home? she thought, and began to move on.

A short way past the crossroads Ruth came to a small garage on her left and glanced in at the first sounds of life that morning. A hammering rang out from the underbelly of a car that was stranded on a hydraulic ramp. Suddenly the hammer hit the ground with a clang and a figure emerged into the light. A dollop of oil had put a black patch over one eye and he cursed as he wiped it away.

Ruth was about to move on when the boy looked up and stared at her so intently that she froze. She had the strange feeling that he was standing directly in front of her, his face almost touching hers. She stared back, sweat trickling icily under her arms.

Still, he stared.

Ruth looked down, bathed in an awkward heat. Thoughts flashed like neon signs.

God, how rude. Who does he think he –? Come on, look up. Stare him out.

Ruth glanced up. He had not moved. She opened her mouth to say something insulting but her mind went blank, so she turned and walked on, scissor-legged. Forget it, she thought, but his face was tattooed on to her memory with jabbing needles of embarrassment. She could picture his prominent forehead, etched with two deep frown lines, and the way his nose fell like a plumbline from jutting brows so that he appeared to be staring out from an early warrior's helmet. His eyes were of a blue that was startling, set against skin brown with more than just a summer tan. He had a wide, sullen mouth, the skin of his lower lip cracked and peeling.

What was he staring at?

Ruth guessed him to be about seventeen, with a stocky body starting to develop the muscles of a man. His thick, dark hair had been badly cut and he was wearing dirty, baggy overalls. He could never be called good-looking, yet something about him had caused a warmth in her insides, a shortening of breath. Ruth winced, remembering.

He didn't seem surprised; like he was expecting me. What, then? He looked as though he felt sorry for me. And he looked . . . scared. Why scared?

She shuddered in the cold wind.

Down at the bottom of the hill, the boy stood just outside the garage gates. One hand worried at his lower lip, picking at the peeling skin, and still he stared. Even when Ruth disappeared over the brow of the hill he stayed, motionless, as though he could still see her.

The coarse smell of the sea became stronger as Ruth approached the school. She licked her lips and caught

8

the taste of salt. Trying to look casual while her heart
jumped in her chest, she walked among the chattering groups converging at the gates.

'Hey,' called a tall blonde to her friend, 'have you
seen Debbie's tan? Looks like the Greek Islands were
sunny.'

'Typical.'

'Yeah. Listen, don't mention it to her. She'll be
dying for us to say how brown she is.'

Ruth came to a halt, shocked by the strange, soft,
Cornish drawl. What if they can't understand what I
say? she thought. What if they laugh? The girls
pushed past on to a tarmac square, flanked on three
sides by the grey stone walls of the school buildings.
A group of boys gathered next to Ruth, oblivious and
talking excitedly.

'Come on, Ryder. You didn't do that.'

'I did.'

'And she let you? She didn't mind?'

'Oh, no. She enjoyed it.'

Lewd sniggers were passed around like cigarettes.
Ruth walked away into the schoolyard, avoiding
footballs and small boys. Their shrieks and yells
bounced off the surrounding walls and were echoed
by seagulls circling above.

Cowering in corners were groups of tiny, black-
blazered first-years, looking immaculate and frightened. A few had dumped their oversized satchels and
loosened their ties and were swaggering about to
show that starting a new school was no big deal.

Right, no big deal, thought Ruth, trying to ignore
the first points and stares.

'Now then, Rachel. My name is Mr Edwards and –'

'Ruth.'

'What?'

'Ruth, sir . . . it's Ruth.'

'Oh.' Mr Edwards looked at the piece of paper in his hand. 'Quite right. Anyway, ah, Ruth, I'm your form tutor and you must come to me if you have any problems, all right?' He smiled at her encouragingly. With his pale, mild eyes and sandy hair, he looked like the kind of person who gets ignored at cheese counters, but Ruth nodded and smiled back. The silence went on a fraction too long. Worry skimmed his face and he floundered in to fill the gap. 'Well . . . ah . . . right. I . . . ah . . . right, if you're ready, it's time for registration. Follow me, Rachel.'

The whole class watched Ruth walk to the only spare seat in the room. She sat down and concentrated on rummaging through her school bag until Mr Edwards managed to persuade everyone to attend to the business of the new school year.

Taking a deep breath, Ruth settled more comfortably into her chair and slid a sideways glance at her neighbour. She saw a pale, neat girl whose fine blonde hair floated in timid wisps around a bland and innocent face. She looked more like a first-year than a fourth-year. She had been peering at Ruth from under white lashes and, as soon as their eyes met, she began to whisper without pausing for breath, as though afraid of being interrupted.

'Hello, my name's Tracey. Mr Edwards asked me to be your guide till you know your way around. Not that there's much to see in a school this size. Not what you're used to, is it?'

'No. I'm Ruth –'

'Yes. I know. That's a biblical name, isn't it? I've

got a cousin called Ruth . . .' Tracey's eager whisper was already becoming an irritation, like static on a radio. She leaned closer, plucking at Ruth's sleeve with a nail-bitten hand. Ruth drew back, repelled by such an intense need to be noticed and liked. She decided to know her way around as quickly as possible.

At break, Tracey took Ruth along to a high-ceilinged cloakroom that was split down the middle by a wall of lockers. Voices floated out from a hidden corner.

'Did you hear her dad's dead?'

'Yeah, heart attack. They've taken over Pengelly's grocery. Mark told me the old miser wouldn't let them move in until the last day of the holiday so he didn't miss out on any of the summer trade.'

'I saw the mother when she was in there looking it over. Fancy her daughter being a skinny redhead. You've got to feel sorry for her, really, haven't you? Perhaps we could –'

'What's the matter with you, Carol? You left the Brownies years ago, remember? I did bring in my photos from Greece, including some of a nudist beach, but since you're all too nosy about her . . .'

'But, Debbie –'

'Where the hell is that pest Tracey? I told her to come straight here with –'

'Shhh.'

Ruth walked round the lockers into a crowd of giggles. For a few seconds no one seemed to know what to do, then a girl elbowed her way to the front. Take me to your leader, thought Ruth as the others fell back. The girl was small and pretty, with dark, silky hair down to her waist. Everything about her

11

was just right, from her neat little feet to her snub nose, and she had the sort of confidence that went with it.

'Hi,' she said. 'My name's Debbie, but you can call me miss.' Her voice was high and sweet but her brown eyes shone maliciously and her white teeth looked sharp, feline. 'What do they call you?' she asked. 'Ginger? Carrot-top? No, seriously,' her face became a mask of sympathy, 'I think you're so brave to walk around like that. How did it happen? You can tell me.'

'How did what happen?'

'Your hair. I thought it must have been an accident. You mean it's meant to look like a – well – like a toilet brush?'

There were dutiful shrieks of laughter and Ruth got ready for a fight, but Debbie defused her own bomb. 'No, I'm only joking, Ruth. Take a seat.'

The day wore on and Ruth knew she was not fitting in. It was like being pushed on stage in the middle of a concert and told to play. The rest of the orchestra had been together for years and the score they used was composed from a common past which she did not share. Ruth tried, but she kept on hitting the wrong note.

Debbie made things worse. Having led the others into playing her tune, she seemed to take delight in keeping Ruth off-key and out of time. She kept up a stream of leading questions, private jokes and ambiguous remarks that were designed to make Ruth look stupid, humourless and short-tempered.

It might even have worked out if Ruth had not resented being there, but she kept comparing it with her old school, and that was a mistake. The buildings were museum pieces, full of cracked tiles, green paint and draughts. The place was small enough to fit into one block of her Coventry comprehensive. Space was so scarce that only the sixth form had a common room and the dining room doubled as a classroom and assembly hall. There was no swimming pool, no theatre and no coffee bar to meet in at the end of the day.

'So, if there's no coffee bar, where do you go after school?' asked Ruth as Tracey hurried her back to the formroom after lunch.

'Home,' said Tracey.

'No, I mean doesn't anything happen in the evenings? No after-school clubs?'

'Oh, we don't have anything like that, except a disco every now and then. They run some clubs at lunchtime but no one stays after the final bell. Lots of us live outside the village, you see, and if we don't catch the school bus at four o'clock, we're stuck. It's a real bind. My house is only fifteen minutes away by car, but it takes the bus hours to go round all the villages and farms. You're lucky, living just down the road . . .'

Tracey scurried on, unaware that Ruth had stopped following and was forcing a way out of the crush at the side of the corridor. Pressed up against a radiator, she stared out of the window at the grey schoolyard, biting her lip.

I'm not staying here, she thought, and the thought would not go away. Instead it grew into an idea. I'm going to get back to Coventry. Perhaps Mum'll find the shop too hard. Or I could go on my own when I'm sixteen . . . Yes. I'm going to go back home.

That afternoon, wariness of the new girl began to

turn into suspicion and dislike. It had always been a delicate balance and Ruth, busy with her plans, stopped trying to swing it her way. She was becoming an outsider. Walking home alone, she suddenly remembered Gary. At her old school they had called him the Flab. Even his pleading eyes, sunk into his face like upholstery buttons in a cushion, had not stopped her from laughing with the others. Now it's my turn to be the fat boy, thought Ruth.

Mrs Davis got through most of the evening meal by pouring a constant stream of words over Ruth's unresponsive head. When she finally ran out of stories about her first day in the shop, she began to ask questions instead.

'So, how was school?'

'Horrible.'

'Oh dear. Never mind. Once the other girls and boys get to know you, you'll have a new set of friends in no time.'

'Mum, why do you always think everything's so simple and cosy? It's not like that. There's this girl . . .' Ruth faltered, at a loss to describe Debbie's subtle, deliberate malice.

'What? She hasn't tried to hurt you, has she?'

'She hasn't touched me, if that's what you mean.'

'Well, you know what to do if she does. Go straight to the teacher. You will, won't you?'

Ruth thought about Mr Edwards and how he had pretended not to see Debbie when she strolled in late at afternoon registration, still listening to her personal stereo. Debbie had not even bothered to glance his way.

'Yes, Mum,' said Ruth.

'Good.' Mrs Davis hesitated. 'You still haven't said anything about the house. What do you think?'

she asked in a bright, careless tone which meant she really cared very much. 'Have you had a good look around?'

'Yes.' Ruth pictured her angular room with a ceiling so high it made the furniture look dwarfish. Then she thought of the draughty old bathroom with a claw-footed bath stuck in the middle of it. She looked around the kitchen at the slab-sided sink and the squat, black, coal-burning stove sulking in a corner. The stone floor was chilling the soles of her feet.

'It's all so – primitive. We're going to freeze this winter.'

'But we can improve it, Ruthie. Get a new bathroom suite, central heating . . .'

'And the living room, it's really poky.'

'Yes, I know. It's because of the alterations. There used to be four big rooms downstairs, just like upstairs, but they knocked two of them together and extended out from the side of the house for the shop. Then they took half of the living room for a store-room. It's not ideal, is it? We could have that as a dining room and convert the third bedroom to an upstairs sitting room.'

'Oh, yes. Central heating, converting rooms – how are you going to pay for it?'

'Don't worry about that; we've got enough. Your dad always insisted on being – Well . . . he . . . we always thought, you know. We always tried to be well insured –'

'You make him sound like a good business deal,' yelled Ruth and ran from the crumpling of her mother's face.

She went to bed early, huddling into the refuge of the sweet-smelling sheets and her faded quilt. She

15

was so tired, her bones ached, but her thoughts kept pacing in restless circles through the day, making her wince each time she recalled Debbie's vicious smile or her mother's plump hands twisting at a handkerchief. Ruth groaned and pushed her forehead hard into the pillow until tiny red spots danced behind her eyelids. She concentrated on watching them until she edged into sleep.

Blackness is pressing in on her. A rough surface is at her back and a smell like putrid meat hangs in the air. Up ahead there is a glimmer of movement and she crawls towards it. Closer – closer – another foot. The figures become clearer and she opens her mouth to shout for help. Then she stops, frowning.

They are gathered in a pale ring, hissing, whispering. They are the size of young children but the shape is – wrong. She catches glimpses of glittering eyes and moist, white skin. Her whole body becomes still and small and silent, but one of them turns and stares over its shoulder.

Straight at her.

Shuffle, scrape, shuffle, they start to move.

'No, you stay where you are. Get back.' Her voice cracks, high and strained.

They move on, towards her.

'You're only a dream,' she whimpers. 'Stop.'

They stop. Her breath sounds harsh in the silence. *What now?* She takes her eyes off them for half a second at a time, glancing left and right. Nothing else moves in the darkness. The tension sings in the air. She watches them, staring into their pale eyes.

Her mind expands until it seems her skull must crack. Then, glowing through the pain like fire through smoke, the words come. She cannot tell whether they are written or spoken; they flicker behind her eyes like hissing neon signs.

'It will be terrible.'

'What will you do?'

'What can you do?'

'Will you try to stop it? We would like that, watching you try to stop it.'

'They will all die.'

She reaches up to block her ears but the words still light up in her head. The creatures gather closer.

She lifts her head and screams. . . .

Ruth was awake. Sweating, shaking, she reached out for the bedside lamp, expecting a claw to close over her wrist. Light flowed over her like a gentle sedative. She was able to sit up but the panic still fluttered in her throat.

It's all right, she told herself. There's nothing to be afraid of. Look, look. There's your chair and your dressing-gown. Don't think of that now. Everything's normal. Look at the light; nothing can get you in the light. The door's shut, the windows are shut. You're safe. Put on the radio. Go on, it's right beside you . . .

The transistor poured out a familiar song at the flick of a switch and only then did Ruth allow herself to think about the dream. She knew it was no ordinary nightmare. Ordinary nightmares were about falling from a great height, or walking to school dressed only in socks, or running through treacle with huge, scaly monsters gaining at every step. No. This one was different.

Was it a warning?

She remembered a couple in the papers who had cancelled their plane tickets because of a dream. The plane they missed had been blown to pieces over the Atlantic.

Ruth frowned and shook her head. *No. They saw what was going to happen. All I saw were those – things. They weren't warning me. More like . . . teasing.* She turned to her curtainless window and shuddered.

Much later, Ruth's bedroom window went dark. In the flat above the garage a light still burned. The boy sat, blinking with tiredness, picking at his lower lip. His sleep had been shattered again but now he had a face to go with the fear. He thought of green eyes and bright hair and wondered what to do.

Chapter Two

The staffroom was stuffy and peaceful. Old notices curled up over the radiator and tobacco smoke lazed against the ceiling. Shouts from the lunchtime schoolyard were as meaningless as the cries of seabirds. Mr Edwards took another bite from a pork pie and spread out his contour maps.

'Idiot,' growled Mr Pugh, hunched over his third-year history essays. His pen scratched its cruel way across the page and retreated to the margin, red nib poised. Peace returned.

Then the door slammed open and hung quivering on its hinges.

'Fresh air,' gasped Mrs Beddows. She swept to the window and flung it wide. Mr Pugh gave a hiss and ground his cigarette butt into submission. Mr Edwards flinched as she sat next to him with a jangle of bracelets.

'Hello, Geoffrey,' she purred.

He blushed and shuffled aside until there was a prim six inches between them. 'Ah, hello Mrs, ah, Beddows.'

'Are you busy?'

'I was just going to prepare a lesson . . .' He

paused hopefully.

'Oh, this won't take long,' she smiled, and leaned towards him, wafting clouds of sandalwood essence.

'Ah, Mrs Beddows –'

'Alice, please. I'd love a coffee and a chat.'

Mr Edwards gave his charts a last, yearning glance and began to poke about beside the kettle, trying to find two clean cups.

'And how can I help you?' he asked, eyebrows rising into question marks.

'Oh, *I* don't need help, Geoffrey. It's the Davis girl.'

'Ah, Rachel.'

'No, Ruth. Ruth Davis. How do you think she's settling down in your form?'

'Well . . .'

'Three weeks now and not even a smile. Quite alone in English, you know. No friends. And those enormous green eyes looking at me.'

'Well, I –'

'That disgustingly popular Debbie creature is having a field day. Don't you think it's unnatural, the way she dominates the whole form? The girl's not sleeping, you know.'

'Well, yes . . .'

'Great potential, they said, but she's not showing it. She just sits there like a sick cat. I know her father died, but that was in January, wasn't it? Now, don't look like that. I'm not being callous – I just think her problems are more, shall we say, immediate. Be a darling, Geoffrey – see what you can do. Now, I must get back to my drama group before the little angels wreck the joint.'

'Yes, I . . . ah . . .' The door was closing before he had even started.

'Shut that window before we all freeze, will you, Edwards?' griped Pugh, lighting up another cigarette.

Ruth caught the flash of sun on a closing window as she stood alone in the schoolyard with her back pressed against the gym wall. She blinked once, tiredly, and chewed at her lower lip. Nineteen, she thought. That was the nineteenth dream last night. She shuddered. Always the same.

What am I supposed to do? Maybe I'm going mad. She pushed her palms hard against the rough stonework and closed her eyes.

'I didn't know you could sleep standing up.'

Ruth jumped. Debbie stood in front of her, flanked by her chosen few.

'Hello,' said Ruth and waited, aching and heavy with tiredness. A girl with hair like oily spaghetti glanced at Debbie, then giggled nervously. Debbie was smiling but her body was tensed like a cat on the hunt. Stretching out a hand, she inspected the nails, slick with crimson varnish.

'I wanted to see you about the disco tonight. We're going. Are you?' The invitation was thrown like a challenge.

'Thanks for asking, but I can't.'

'Oh?'

'See you, then.' Ruth tried to pass but the girls blocked her way.

'What's the excuse this time – washing your hair, are you?' asked Debbie, her tone full of cold mockery.

21

'I've got homework.' So tired, too tired, wailed a voice in her head.

'Is that all?'

No, wailed the voice. My dad's dead, my mum's working a sixteen-hour day and acting like everything's great, and I'm waiting for the world to end.

'It's got to be done tonight,' said Ruth.

'Told you,' cried Debbie, torn between spite and triumph. 'Told you she wouldn't.'

'Rotten snob,' growled Spaghetti-hair, taking a step forward. The bell echoed across the yard and Ruth pushed her way through, heading for the entrance.

'Right, that's it,' Debbie spat. 'Mick! Darren! Come here.'

Ruth fought through the scrum at the door and was halfway down the corridor before the calls started.

'Hoy, randy Ruth. Who's the lucky man tonight, then?'

'Come off it, Mick. She couldn't get fixed up if she advertised.'

'Yeah, her nose'd poke his eye out if he tried to kiss her.'

Ruth walked along the red stone floor while insults wove between the peeling paint and the smell of disinfectant. Once or twice she winced, but it was like throwing a match at someone already in flames. They soon gave up.

Thursday brought the letter. The neat brown envelope was propped against the toast rack when Ruth came downstairs. The smell of porridge turned her stomach and she pushed her plate away.

'Aren't you hungry?' Her mother's voice was sharp

with worry and Ruth glanced up in surprise. In the weeks since the move, Mrs Davis had constructed a smiling mask and hidden inside it, leaving a blank space behind the eye-holes. Now the mask was gone. Ruth looked again at the envelope, trying to catch clues.

'I said, aren't you hungry?'

Ruth shook her head.

'Did you sleep through the night?'

Ruth shook her head a second time. Twenty-one today, she thought, and grimaced.

'Nightmares again?' asked her mother. 'You've got great bruises under your eyes –' She stopped herself, poured a cup of tea and nudged it over. Then she took a deep breath and announced, 'There's a letter come – from the school.' There was a touch of awe in her voice. 'Go on, read it.'

Ruth stared at Mr Edwards' handwriting, which was squashed apologetically into the middle of the page. She saw the words '. . . unsettled . . . concerned . . . lack of friends . . .', then she put the letter back on the table, face down.

'You can't have read it that fast.'

'Enough to get the idea.'

'I'm going up there this lunchtime. Just for a chat.'

Ruth absorbed the careful words without a flicker of emotion. Dark eyed, she stared at the film on her cooling tea. As her mother leaned forward, it shivered into fragments, reflecting greasy smudges of colour in the autumn sunlight, like oil on a wet road.

'Can't you tell me what's wrong, Ruthie? What is it? Is it the school? They're not picking on you, are they?'

Ruth jerked her head slightly, as though away from an irritating fly.

Taking a deep breath, her mother tried again. 'If it's –'

'If you hadn't dragged me down here –' Ruth stopped. This was a road travelled many times before. Both acknowledged the dead-end and turned back.

'I was going to say, if it's your dad – you mustn't try to hide it. I mean, I know I don't usually like any fuss, but don't hide your feelings just to – We ought to – Oh, I don't know what to say . . .' Her mother's face was strained; the fat cheeks quivering with tension. Ruth took in the smudged lipstick and dapples of grey in the dark hair. Love swelled achingly in her throat and she tried, really tried, to explain.

'It's . . .' *What can I say? I'm having these nightmares and they're going to come true? No.* '. . . it's nothing.'

Mrs Davis drew back, hurt. Her mouth hardened. 'Well, I've made an appointment at the doctor's for tonight. Perhaps he can sort you out.'

School was long over by the time Ruth left the cloakroom that afternoon. The building was quiet except for her footsteps and the distant clatter of cleaners. A smell of pine floated down the empty corridors. She reached her formroom, wiped the sweat from her palms and opened the door.

'Ah, Rach . . . er . . . Ruth. Thank you for coming. Do take a seat. That's it.' Mr Edwards did not leave the safety of his desk but he moved round and perched awkwardly on its edge to show that the occasion was informal. 'As you know, I, ah, saw your mother this lunchtime. We were talking about your, ah, problems at school.'

'What problems are they, sir?'

'Ah, well, you know . . .' He gave an embarrassed smile and Ruth stared at a morsel of food that was wedged between his front teeth. 'Well, for instance, your old school sent us such a glowing report, and yet your work here . . .' He shrugged and a sour-sweet mixture of stale sweat and cheap talcum powder wafted her way. 'It's not your best work, is it?'

'I don't know. Sir.'

Mr Edwards tried another tack. 'Your mother told me about your nightmares. What do you think is causing them?'

Silence lay at their feet. Ruth concentrated on the carvings in the desk lid.

'Perhaps the people at school? Debbie can be . . . ah . . . Possibly you miss your friends in Coventry?'

Ruth glanced up. A snail trail of sweat glistened on his upper lip and he kept tugging at his tie.

'Perhaps your father . . . ?'

'My dad –' Ruth began, and was surprised by tears, – is not to blame, she thought fiercely.

'There, there,' muttered Mr Edwards. 'There, there. We thought that must be at the root of it. Your mother thought you might be, ah, starting to get over it, but the move stirred it all up again. Well, that's understandable; moving to a new area is difficult at the best of times, isn't it?

'Your mother told me you were very, ah, close to your father. She said you always went to him for help or advice. It must be hard for you now.'

Ruth did not answer. She thought her mother had already said enough for them both.

Mr Edwards took a deep breath and began to talk again, pronouncing each word carefully, as though it might burn the sides of his mouth. 'Now, Rachel, what we decided, your mother and I, was to leave things for a while in the hope that you might be able to, ah, sort yourself out. However, we want you to know that if there are any problems you can't discuss with your mother, or any time you want help with homework, or just a coffee and a chat – well, you know where to find me.'

Understanding drove into her skull like a nail. She looked down at her fists. *I'm going to stand up and tip that box of chalks over his stupid, chattering head . . .*

Pink, blue and green dust stuck to the sweat on his face.

'You moron. You think you can replace my dad when you can't even remember my name?' Her desk turned over easily, making a satisfying clatter. She walked to the row of potted plants on the windowsill.

'This is for being so stupid –' The first plant smashed to the floor, scattering soil over an impossible distance.

'No, not my flowering cactus,' pleaded Mr Edwards, but the second pot fell.

'– and that's for the way you smell. And this is for looking like a slug in a suit –'

. . . But Mr Edwards had stopped talking and was looking with mild concern at the pale, motionless girl sitting in front of him. Her breathing was quick and shallow, featherlight, and she stared fixedly at her clenched fists.

'Rachel? Are you all right?' Ruth glanced up. The box of chalks sat demurely on the desk top and the plants stood in line on the windowsill.

'Yes. I'm all right.' She smiled tightly. A teacher was, after all, a teacher.

'Fine. Well, glad that's sorted out. I'll see you tomorrow, when you start getting to grips with all that school work. Good night, then.' He left the room with a jaunty spring to his step and Ruth suddenly understood how bewildering life must be for him. A hard fist of sadness settled in her chest, like the first time she had caught her mother in a lie; the first time she had realised her father was afraid.

'Well, I'm glad that's sorted out,' echoed her mother as they left the doctor's surgery that evening. 'I thought Doctor Pascoe was very nice. His daughter's at your school, isn't she? Do you know her?'

'Yes,' said Ruth, remembering how the man's dark, darting eyes and neat, sharp features had reminded her of Debbie. He had prescribed sleeping tablets without even looking her way.

A dull rattling sounded across the courtyard of the garage as they passed and Ruth glanced inside. A figure was sliding shut the huge double doors of the repair shop.

Don't, don't, don't, she pleaded silently, but he stopped, swinging round as though she had shouted his name through the dusk.

'Ben! Come and get this tea, boy.' He stared for one, two, three seconds more before turning and heading for the tiny garage office.

'Who was that? Do you know him?'

'No.'

'Are you sure? He gave you a real good stare –'

'Mum, I don't know him. OK?'

'Hmmm. Ben, that man called him, wasn't it?'

Ben, yes, Ben. The name had flown through the

27

dark air and nested in her head. 'I really didn't notice.'

'There's been gossip about him in the shop.'

'Oh, has there.' Ruth made her words drip with boredom.

'Yes. They didn't seem to like him much.'

'Who're they? The village mafia?'

'Now, Ruth. They're all good customers, especially old Mr Tamblyn. He never shops anywhere else.'

'Only because you let him get away with all that shoplifting while Mrs Penhale is meant to be distracting you.'

'But he never takes much, only the odd pack of biscuits. And he is a pensioner, you know.'

'Oh, come on, Mum. You don't do it out of kindness. If you got the police on to those four, you'd never hear the end of it; they're a village institution. I think we're the only people here who aren't related to one of them. You know we'd go out of business if we shopped them, and they know it too. It's a sort of polite blackmail. They'd never believe it back in Coventry if I told them there's only one street gang here and you've got to be over sixty before you can join.'

'Get any sharper and you'll cut yourself,' snapped Mrs Davis and instantly regretted it. That was the most her daughter had said to her for weeks.

Ruth managed to stay awake until the stars shone as hard and bright as lasers, and fishermen were easing their boats away from sleeping harbours. The tablets stood untouched on her bedside table. I've beaten them tonight, she thought, and was swamped by a wave of sleep.

The smell dredges up a childhood memory of a dead jellyfish baking on the hot sand. She remembers how she pierced the taut skin with a stick, releasing an oily, surging stink that filled her lungs. Now the same smell hangs in the air.

She keeps her eyes closed. Wake – up – now. Her brain pulses with effort. Lights dance behind her lids. She counts to five, slowly, and opens her eyes. No bedroom. Dead-jellyfish smell and clammy fear. Glimmers of white over to the left, moving in.

They'll stop soon. They always stop, she thinks, watching the bleached shapes inch closer through the darkness. A touch, sliming across her lips, makes her jerk back, cracking her head against rock. Eggshell, she thinks, as acid pain fills her mouth.

'What are you doing?' she whispers, stupidly shocked at the break in routine. They lean forward, stroking her with wet, boneless fingers.

'What are you?' she screams, and they show her. Darkness still surrounds them but they seem to become floodlit from within. They are children only in size, with pallid bodies less than four feet high. Their heads are big, with sparse wisps of hair clinging like red-grey fungus to their scalps. In their dried-up, old men's faces, wet mouths stretch wide like slits. Their teeth are filed to points. Worst of all are the eyes; they are like the eyes of reptiles, but they burn with a pale fire, and the pupils are thin splinters of coal.

Her spine is crushed hard against rock, but her legs still scrabble to push herself away from the creatures. Her scream vibrates on the air like

29

stretched wire. She opens her mouth to scream again, but they all turn away and stare into the shadows with their lizard eyes. Tense, expectant, listening.

It is the sort of noise that starts imperceptibly, like an approaching train. Soon it grows from a whisper to a rumble, welling up all around them. Everything, even the solid floor, begins to shudder – then the power dwindles and turns in on itself, muttering.

'See,' the voices rasp in her mind, 'see. It has started.'

'You cannot stop it now.'

'We have disturbed the beast.'

'It is awake. It will grow in strength.'

She tries to breathe again but has forgotten how. Her heart is pushing great, slow surges of blood to her head. The blood wails in her ears, blotting out the voices, and she begins to spiral down towards the ground . . .

Ruth fought her way out of twisted sheets, body slick with sweat. Weak, grey light seeped through the curtains, turning the room into a grainy newspaper photograph. She sobbed, once, then sat up, shivering, to wait for morning.

'Take the day off, love, you look a bit peaky,' said her mother at breakfast. 'Periods, is it?'

'No,' said Ruth, but Mrs Davis wasn't listening. The mask was back in place. Ruth was fine; everything was fine. Just how Brian had always wanted it.

'Yes, a nice hot-water bottle and a day in the warm'll soon solve that,' she said, turning from the sink. Ruth got up and walked out of the room.

'Ruthie . . . ?' A tiny spasm skittered across her mother's face. She moved to the mirror and stared at her reflection. The dark hair was set like a crash helmet but still she patted it softly with the palm of her hand. She eased her wedding ring back on to a finger grown too plump for it and pulled on a pink checked overall. A final nod, a vague smile and she moved to the shop door. So ordinary; so alone.

Ruth stood at the spare-bedroom window, dressed in jeans and her favourite emerald green sweater. The late-September sun shone in a disinterested way. Chimneys flew ragged flags of smoke and birds blew across the clear blue sky like scraps of cindered paper. Suddenly, Ruth wanted to walk, far enough to make her legs ache. She hurried downstairs to cut some sandwiches.

The narrow farm road to the cliffs meandered through stretches of bracken where goats were tethered. White, piebald, black, they chewed incessantly and stared with yellow eyes as she passed. The road climbed to a row of sturdy white coastguards' cottages and came to a halt in a gravelled circle just behind the lighthouse.

Ruth turned left and followed the clifftop path. To her right the grass ended in a startling plunge of granite cliffs. They ranged in colour from blue-black to a dull ash grey and spray gave the lower rocks a diamond glitter. The sea gnawed at the cliff base and alluvial tin, swept down by rain and rivers, danced on the foam like the earth's blood.

Ruth walked until she reached one of the bleak, narrow ruins that stood on the skyline. Roofless and slowly crumbling, it was supported by a tall, round chimney at one side. Two blank, arched windows, set

31

one above the other, made her think of the shell of the old Coventry cathedral.

Close to, the grey stone was softened by lichen, and flowers grew from the crevices. Ruth found a sheltered spot and sat down to eat. There was a constant background sigh of wind and sea, punctuated by seagull cries. A flurry of them were besieging a fishing boat as it inched its way along the horizon. She rested her head against the rough grey stone and watched the boat head doggedly for home.

'Hello.'

Ruth dropped the sandwich and turned her head so sharply, her neck bones clicked. 'Oh, it's you,' she said, as though she knew him. 'I . . . I mean . . .' and she looked out to sea again, cheeks burning.

Ben stood, scowling and silent.

'Um, you work at the garage, don't you?'

'Yes.'

Wonderful, thought Ruth.

Ben shifted his weight and stuffed his hands deeper into his jeans' pockets.

'I'm Ruth Davis. We just moved into the shop a few weeks ago –'

'I know.'

Oh, God, thought Ruth. 'I – I came to see what this ruin was, but I'm still not sure.'

'Engine house. For the old tin mines.'

'Oh. That's interesting. Well,' she started to get to her feet, 'I'd better be getting back –'

'No. I wanted to talk to you.'

Ruth hesitated, then moved over to give him room to sit down.

'Sandwich?' she asked. A broad hand, broken-nailed and stained with oil, reached over and took the

32

last one. She risked a sideways glance. His dark-blue eyes were staring straight ahead as he chewed. He looked furious.

The silence stretched until Ruth could think of no words big enough to fill the gap. She concentrated on keeping her right arm and leg still, to avoid brushing against him accidentally. Her knee was just beginning to twitch uncontrollably when he spoke again.

'It's about last night.'

Ruth stared. 'What?'

'Is something frightening you?' The words came out in a painful rush. He would not look at her but began to stab at the earth with a sharp-edged stone.

'How did you know?'

Ben turned to her at last, eyes wide with relief. 'You mean I'm right?'

'I've been having – dreams.'

'And last night, was it worse than usual?' The furious look was gone now; his face was open, younger.

Ruth nodded.

'Yes, I knew it was. I've been waking up. The first time, I didn't know why. Then you walked past on your way to school and I knew straight away.'

'How? How did you know?'

'I don't know; I just knew. And I was right, wasn't I? You being scared is what woke me up, see. Like someone screaming right in my ear. But I couldn't think what to do. I mean, suppose I'd been wrong? I thought –'

'– you might be going mad,' finished Ruth and they shared a look of recognition.

'So, last night . . . ?'

33

'Yes,' Ruth croaked. 'They're worse than night-mares. Last night was awful.'

'Maybe I can help.'

Ruth drew a shaky breath and began. At first, she was careful, watching for a raised eyebrow or a twitch of the lips, but soon she was lost in the horror of her story and the relief of telling it.

Ben studied her as she talked. She was so thin. Her bones seemed too large for her skin, angling out everywhere. Her voice moved steadily through the nightmares, but her body was trying to pack itself away into the smallest possible space. By the time the telling was finished, she was crouched over with her knees drawn up to her chest and her arms wrapped tightly around her ankles.

'That's it,' she said.

'So, you think these creatures have disturbed something very powerful and it's going to cause a disaster –'

'But I don't know what it'll be. It's horrible – I can't even warn anyone.' Her face was a white triangle. She didn't seem to notice her fingernails digging into her ankles.

'Hold on. Sure they're not just dreams?'

'Oh, yes. It's the same thing again and again, and the creatures are too real. I mean, I can even smell them. They're premonitions.'

'Or echoes.'

'What?'

'Well, you must be sending out pretty strong fear signals to wake me up after a hard day's work, so you're obviously a good telepath –'

'I'm not a telepath!'

Ben sighed. 'Don't be daft. Everyone's telepathic.

Or would you rather I said sensitive? Or intuitive? Sixth sense? Instinct? Everyone's sending out and picking up signals all the time; we all get feelings about people or places. It's just that some people are more receptive than others.'

'But this has never happened to me before.'

'Exactly. You've never been here before, have you? Which brings me back to echoes. Even if these dreams are something stronger than nightmares, it doesn't mean you're having premonitions. What if you're picking up on something that's already happened? We're not short on death and disaster round here, you know. We're up to our ears in old stories and legends. The tourists love it.'

'So?'

'So, maybe because you're new to the place, you're picking up what most people miss. Like a dog can hear those high-pitched whistles. Like Walter de la Mare; I was reading something about him the other week. Don't look so surprised. Just because I work in a garage, it doesn't mean I'm stupid. I know more about the place I was born in than all those idiots at your school – and I didn't have it spoon-fed.'

Ruth blinked. 'What? Did I look . . . ? I'm sorry. I didn't mean – If I looked surprised it's because – this whole thing –'

'OK, forget it. Walter de la Mare came to Cornwall once. He started getting scared as soon as they crossed the border. The further in the coach travelled, the worse he got. Cold sweats, white face, the lot. Wouldn't say what was wrong, though. It was as though he saw things outside the coach windows that no one else could see. He wouldn't stay the night. The coachman had to turn around and they didn't rest the horses until they were back over the county line. Do you see what I mean? Echoes.'

'Yes. But I really think it's more than that. All the time I keep thinking, I've got to warn them – but I don't know who to warn.'

'Right, so we'll treat them as premonitions. We'd better decide what to do.'

'But – we can't do anything.'

'Not much of a fighter, are you? Giving up just because the odds are against you. There must be something we can do.'

'Well, I did think – if I could just find the place in these dreams. If it exists, I think I would know it straight away.'

'I thought you said it was too dark to see anything?'

'Yes, but I would know just by the feel of it, I think. A bit like a metal detector. But we'd have to have a plan: sectioning off a map, or something.'

'It's worth a try. What if we pick likely places, the ones in local legends? I'll see what I can find in the old stories and make a list. Right, I must get back to work,' he added, jumping to his feet. 'I'll call, when I've got a list started.' Without another word, he turned and walked off.

'Yes, fine,' she called to his retreating back. 'You go on. I'll walk back alone.' The cliff path disappeared into a gulley and he followed it without looking back. 'So nice to have met you!' yelled Ruth, throwing her sandwich crust after him.

'So much for a knight in shining whatsit,' she grumbled, but her irritation would not stay. The prospect of action was like a signpost in a strange city. Ruth lay back in the bracken with the sun on her face, and slept.

Chapter Three

Night was edging the sky as Ruth reached home. Her mother, framed in the shop doorway, was peering down the street.

'Where've you been? I was starting to get worried.'

'I told you I was going for a walk along the cliffs.'

'All day?'

'Well, no. I stopped for some sandwiches and then . . . it was so quiet and sunny, I just fell asleep.'

'Ruthie! Honestly, you've got a perfectly good bed upstairs. And you can't be too careful these days. Still, you look like it's done you some good. Come on inside, then. I've got something for you.'

A large cardboard box sat next to the stove in the kitchen.

'There you are. Your dad always said we'd have one if we moved down here. I can't get it to come out of the box, though. You have a try while I lock up.'

As soon as the door closed, a head periscoped above the straw. It was glossy red with a nose like a fruit gum and enormous wet brown eyes. They exchanged a brief, surprised look, then the puppy gave a yelp and shot back into the box.

Ruth drew up a chair and sat down. 'Hello, you,'

she said, and began to talk, soft and low.

By the end of the evening he was wobbling about the room, sniffing like an old man with no manners and peeing against the table leg. He had trouble controlling his paws, which looked like outsize orange fun-fur slippers stuck on the end of his spindly legs.

'Big paws means he's going to be a big dog. That's what your dad liked about red setters. He thought they were so tall and elegant.'

'Elegant!' spluttered Ruth, watching him trip over thin air yet again. 'Oh, come here. I'm not really laughing at you.'

When she put her arms around him, he hid his soft muzzle under her armpit and sighed. His coat was like silk, his heart beat fast against his ribs and he smelled of fresh straw. Ruth was sold.

For two nights her sleep was calm and on Sunday afternoon she met Alison Bowden as she walked through the drizzling village with her puppy. Alison was nearly six feet tall, with short blonde hair and eyes the colour of rainclouds. She moved with a graceful ease, never seeming to hurry, and she was the best scientist in the school.

'Well, hello, Ruth,' she said. 'Isn't he beautiful? What's he called?'

'Rusty.'

'Because of his colour?'

'And because he pees over everything in sight.'

Alison laughed. 'I'm glad I met you. My parents are asleep in front of the telly and I was getting so bored. Why don't you come back for a coffee?'

'But – he's not house-trained.'

'That's OK, it's lino in the kitchen. Come on.'

Her home was a tiny terraced house with two downstairs rooms. She took them through the back yard into a warm kitchen with a gas fire hissing against the wall. Dancing blue light, gunfire and a man's snores leaked from the front room. Alison smiled. 'Is there life after Sunday dinner?' she whispered.

Rusty sprawled in front of the fire, the coffee was strong and hot, and soon they were talking about school.

'All my marks are bad,' said Ruth. 'And that Debbie –'

'Yes, I know. I can understand it, though.'

'What?'

'She sees you as a rival.'

'Me?'

'Yes, you. The big-city girl. The new face. School's the only place she has any power, you see, and power's important to Debbie. She doesn't get much attention at home.'

'You're not trying to tell me she's neglected? Her dad's a doctor and her mum teaches. They must be loaded.'

'That's true, but they don't take much notice of her. If they listen to anyone, it's her younger brother. I remember one day when I went there after school. Her dad was in the kitchen trying to figure out the dials on their new washing machine. "Hello, dear," he said, "how was school?" "OK," said Debbie. "The roof fell in, the student teacher made passionate love to me in the book cupboard and one kid died after eating the rice pudding." "Good, good," said her dad, and he went right on fiddling with the washing machine.'

'Well, I can't accept all that poor little rich girl stuff. Neglect means no one to care what you wear, or whether you're clean; that sort of thing. She's just got a nasty personality.'

'Maybe. But she'd feel less threatened if you tried to be a bit more friendly.'

'Me?'

'Yes, you! Tell you what, why don't you walk in with me tomorrow, and we'll take it from there?'

When Ruth left Alison's house, the night air smelled of wet gardens. The steamy windows of the pub shook with rowdy singing, while a stream of cold, soaring notes flowed from the Methodist Chapel next door.

A new start tomorrow. Yes, that would be . . . But what about Debbie? I could give it a try. I wish Alison didn't remind me of a social worker. No, that's not fair. Oh, but, back to normal. That would be . . .

Ruth reached the crossroads and stopped under a streetlight. Raindrops played a complicated rhythm on the tin tables outside the tea shop. To her right, the dark road swept up past her house to the moors. To her left, it curled towards the cliffs and ended at the lighthouse. The school was down that road, and the garage with Ben's flat above. Ruth stood in the hissing darkness, wondering which way to turn.

Perhaps they are just nightmares. All that talk about telepathy and legends – Alison would laugh. He knew about the dreams, though. How do I explain that?

Rusty's eyes glowed red as he looked up at her, haloed in a fine fuzz of rain. He was shivering. 'OK,

40

boy. Let's go home,' said Ruth, and they turned away from the garage, up the dark moors' road.

'Don't worry,' whispered Alison at the school gates. 'Everyone loves a prodigal. It reaffirms their faith in themselves.'

'Velly wize, master,' said Ruth. 'Look, the only way I'm going to get anywhere today is through you. They all respect you.'

'OK. But don't sit there looking at them as though they were cow-pats. Show an interest and join in the conversation.'

'Have I been that bad?'

'Yes. But you've had a lot on your mind, haven't you?'

Ruth blinked. 'What do you mean?'

'Well, losing your dad and leaving your friends behind.'

'Oh. Yes.'

'We'll start at registration. Edwards is supposed to lead a daily debate on issues of importance, but we've cured him of that. He usually lets us chat. And don't worry. This lot'll soon come round if you treat them nicely.'

Ruth was right about Alison. People trusted her. She was the balance of Debbie in other things as well as looks. Debbie was all cruel excitements, but Alison was cool water on a hot day. When she sat down with Ruth beside her and began to talk, they were willing to be drawn. Ruth smiled until her face ached and the group thawed until even Debbie joined in. Ruth felt ridiculously pleased; it had been cold standing alone.

★

'Coming down the main street for some lunch?' asked Debbie.

Ruth hesitated slightly before she nodded, smiling. Alison had gone to the science lab and something had changed. Nothing outwardly seemed to be different but they all knew the safety catch was off the gun and Debbie was the trigger.

'Carol's mum serves at the baker's,' said Debbie, linking arms with Spaghetti-hair as they left the school, 'and there's usually a few extras for special friends.' Spaghetti-hair went pink with pleasure.

So that's her use, thought Ruth.

Debbie stopped at the garage, just before the cross-roads. 'Shall we call on Ben?' she asked, and Ruth blinked with surprise. Debbie was grinning, showing her small, white teeth, and the others started to snigger. They clustered at the entrance to the fore-court; hunters after some sport.

'Ben? Oh Be-en . . .'

'Yoo-hoo . . .'

'How's the old IQ, Ben?'

'Have they asked for you at Cambridge yet?'

'Hey, Treseder, how many wheels on a car? That's not a multi-choice question.'

Ruth winced. The meaning of this performance was lost on her but the tone was clear. The school, as well as the village, seemed to be against him.

Pale little Tracey Penrose was standing at the back of the group, biting her nails. 'What's this all about?' asked Ruth.

'Oh, nobody likes him because he always acts as though he's better than anyone else but the truth is he was in my brother's class last year and he left without even taking his exams –' Tracey paused for a short breath before rushing on. 'They're always teasing him about it because it makes him really mad and –'

'Oh, come on,' said Debbie, turning away. 'He isn't going to show. Never mind, Ruth.'

'What do you mean?'

'Well, you are going out with him, aren't you?'

There it was: Debbie's special skill. Homing in on a weak spot like a heat-seeking missile. She folded her arms, raised an eyebrow and glanced around the uncertain faces before turning back to Ruth. 'You weren't the only one away on Friday. You were seen. On the cliffs. With Ben Treseder.'

Ruth felt as though Debbie had snatched her bedclothes on a cold night. All she wanted was to be warm again. 'I – I was walking by myself – he just came along and started talking. He wasn't invited. He wasn't even wanted.' Ruth could hear herself; pleading, desperate. She felt sick.

'Really?' Seconds crawled by, then Debbie decided. 'You poor thing. He can be a real pain, that kid.' She linked arms with Ruth and turned towards the crossroads.

As soon as they reached the main street, Ruth spotted him. Dirty blue overalls, hands rammed into the pockets. A scowl on his face and oil on his cheek.

Oh hell. What do I do?

'Look what's coming,' crowed Debbie, tightening her grip. Ben saw the group and scowled even harder.

Perhaps he won't see me. Let him just walk past . . .

He was only a few strides away when he recognised her and smiled. Brown skin, white teeth. In slow motion, Ruth stretched her face into a grin, turned to Debbie and said, 'New fashion is it, baggy overalls?' Debbie began to laugh with high-pitched shrieks and everyone joined in like a flock of gulls. Ruth watched his eyes turn to black stone. His smile snapped off and he walked past without faltering.

'Off to the cliffs again, are you?' screeched Debbie. 'Hoping to find some other girl to bother? You meet some real weirdos up there these days.'

'Yeah.'

'Some people never know when they're not wanted.'

'Yeah.'

'Why don't you go home and play with your spanner, Ben Treseder?'

'Yeah, go on.'

'Yeah.'

Ben turned the corner and was gone.

Thursday was the night of the next school disco. Ruth stood at the mirror in her favourite jeans and a soft, moss-green T-shirt with a slashed neck. It was loose enough to disguise the fact that she had breasts like orange pips and it brought out the green of her eyes. 'Not bad, Davis,' she murmured, and set off to call for Alison.

Alison answered the door wearing a pair of grey pinstripe trousers that did wonders for her long legs, and a white, tight-fitting waistcoat with no shirt underneath. Her shoes, beads and bag were scarlet and her fair hair shone softly in the early-evening light. The effect was stunning.

'You're meant to say hello,' said Alison.

'You look – I'd look like Charlie Chaplin if I tried that, but you look great.'

'Thanks – Oxfam shop again. Shall we go?'

Music was already pounding from the school hall

and a sixth-former was selling tickets at the door. He eyed Alison appreciatively as he took their money. 'Well, well. It's Fred Astaire and Ginger Rogers,' he said, ruffling Ruth's hair. 'Where've you left your top hat?'

'Right over there next to your bath chair,' said Alison, smiling sweetly. 'Fred Astaire, I ask you,' and she swept through the door without a backward glance.

In the hall all the curtains were closed but they didn't quite meet in the middle and dust motes danced in the shafts of setting sun. They were the only things dancing; the floor was deserted. Mr Barker the art teacher sat on the stage, wearing a sweatshirt that said 'Dragon Disco'. He had two decks, a box full of singles and six coloured light-bulbs that flashed spasmodically. There was a strong smell of gym shoes.

'Smart, isn't it?' yelled Barry Curnow, coming in behind Ruth. 'You know what's happening? This is a herd of lesser-spotted Cornish wallies about to begin their courtship rituals. It's traditional for the males and females to stand apart on the edges of the clearing for the first hour. That's your side over there. See you later.'

By ten o'clock the place was unrecognisable. The dark air was soaked in sweat and perfume. Debbie, long hair swinging, high breasts bouncing, was the centre of attention. Alison and the sixth-former were cheek to cheek and the only clear space on the floor was around Mr Edwards, who was twisting sharply from left to right and jerking his arms like a demented drummer-boy.

'Get off, will you?' snapped Ruth at the fifth-year

45

breathing beery fumes down her neck. He had staggered up half an hour earlier and said, 'Hi, I'm Ian Ryder, but you can call me sir.' He had blond hair and perfect teeth. Ruth knew he had perfect teeth because he smiled a lot, especially when he was trying to get a hand up her T-shirt or inside her jeans.

'I said, get off!'

'I thought you were a sophisticated city girl,' he yelled. 'Glue sniffing, sex parties and all that?'

'You call that sophisticated?'

Ian was about to answer when a boy grabbed his arm. Ruth heard, '. . . vodka . . . nicked . . . Dad won't miss it . . .' and Ian took off without another word.

Soon Mr Pugh took to prowling the edges of the hall and leaping into darkened classrooms with his torch. He ran for the light switches at ten-thirty like a runner for the tape.

Ruth passed Ian Ryder on her way home. He was bent over in the gutter, retching. 'Very sophisticated, Ian,' she said, giving him a wide berth. She scurried past the garage without looking up and reached home with her ears still ringing from the music.

'Did you think it was finished?'

She opens her eyes to a familiar, heavy darkness. The creatures grin in welcome, their pointed teeth glistening with spit. 'We wouldn't break our promises.'

'We told you it had started.'

'They will all die.'

The floor quivers as something hugely heavy begins to move. The creatures laugh; a sound

46

like acid on metal. Her stomach clenches at the stench of their breath.

'Please . . .'

A deep moan becomes a roar and a pounding weight slams nearer, with an age between each step.

'Listen. The power grows.'

They stare off into the darkness and she climbs to her feet, starts to back away. Silently she turns and moves on, hands outstretched. Leathery blackness wings about her. On and on in shuffling inches, leaving them behind.

Keep going. Keep going.

She reaches towards a glimmer of light and screams as her hands touch something soft and clammy. Her arms are gripped. She is dragged back and held upright in the darkness, ready to meet whatever moves towards them.

Friday morning, smudge-eyed, Ruth was passing the garage on the way to school when Ben stepped into her path.

'You dreamed again.'

She nodded and looked down, following the pale stretch of a drowned worm as it floated past in the gutter. Silence fell like snow.

'Ben, last Monday –'

'You'd better hurry up before your little pals arrive.'

' – I –'

'No, there's nothing to say, is there?'

'But, listen, about the dreams. The doctor said they were down to moving to a new place and my dad's death.' It sounded pathetic, even as she said it.

Ben laughed. 'Why did the dreams stop for a week? You thought the two of us might be able to do something, didn't you? Perhaps those creatures sensed that and wanted to split us, so they eased off just long enough to make you feel safe again.'

'No.' Ruth sidestepped but he stepped with her.

'Perhaps they can even get to other people. What about your mother buying that puppy? Something to divert you. Bit of a coincidence, wasn't it? And those twits at school, so friendly all of a sudden.'

'It wasn't like that.'

'Ruth, we can't just ignore it –'

'We?' Ruth was suddenly flaring with anger. 'We? I've only met you once – who are you to tell me what to do?'

'I'm the one who wakes up in the night when you're frightened, remember? Wait –'

'You let go of my arm, now!'

'Ruth –'

'Are you going to let go of my arm,' hissed Ruth in a cold, tight voice, 'or do I have to kick you where it hurts?'

'Just hear me out. If you come to your senses by tomorrow, meet me here at nine-thirty. We've got places to visit.'

'I wouldn't go anywhere with you.'

'Hey, let go of her!'

Ben glanced up, startled, to see Debbie at the front of a group of fourth-years. He turned back to Ruth with a shrug of dismissal.

'Go on, lads,' yelled Debbie. A fist slammed into his belly and he doubled over, gasping. Ruth was pushed back against the garage wall. 'Stay there,' ordered Debbie. 'We'll take care of him.' She darted back to the fight with a fierce joy on her face and Ruth thought, I'm not the reason for this, I'm just an excuse.

They all went for him. It was the release of years of hostility. There was spit on his face, a boot in his kidneys and a fist in his hair – then a knee caught him across the nose.

Ruth watched Ben fall and she began to shake. It was oddly quiet. Just dull thuds, the scrape of shoes and noisy breathing.

'No, don't,' she whispered, without knowing it.

Then the scrum bulged outwards and suddenly Ben was standing again. Blood ran from his nose and rage made his face chalky white. 'You bastards,' he rasped, and began to slam his fists into anyone near enough. He was two years older than they, with muscles used to work, and soon there were more watchers than fighters. A few more stepped back and Ben stood alone in a grey square, pulling harsh breaths from the air.

'Anyone for more?' Ben waited for a move but none came. They just stared, their faces sour with hate. In the face of so much bitterness and intolerance, he suddenly looked very tired. His shoulders slumped and his face crumpled. Ruth couldn't understand why he was crying. He had won, hadn't he? She ached with shame for him and looked away. No one seemed to know what to do.

Debbie broke the spell. 'That's revolting. That's really disgusting. A big boy like him.'

Spaghetti-hair laughed in a loud, forced way and others joined her, glad to fill the uneasy silence.

'You just keep away from her now, right? Or you'll

really have something to cry about.'

Ben pushed a way through and headed for the garage, slapping the tears from his face. Their jeers followed him.

'Come back for some more, grease-monkey.'

'Next time we won't just bloody your nose, we'll break it.'

'There you are, Ruth,' crowed Debbie. 'Problem solved.'

But Ruth knew better.

The sun crawled over the rooftops and peered blearily at Ruth standing against the garage wall. When the yard gate opened she jumped, then became very still. Ben walked towards her, with one eye bruised and a swelling over the bridge of his nose.

'Hello,' she shrilled, beaming like a politician.

'So, you've turned up. Alone? Or are the heavies round the corner?'

'Ben, I –'

'Let's be clear about something. If you go back to those cretins after today and tell them I've been pestering you again . . . if you cut me dead in the street in front of them –'

'No! No, I won't.'

'What did you tell them? Was I cast as the cliffside sex maniac or the village idiot? Did you all have a good laugh?'

'Ben, I'm so sorry –'

'Sorry!'

'It was the first time they'd been friendly to me for weeks.'

'So you went running like a little dog.'

'No, it wasn't like that. They . . . I . . . Debbie is

50

so clever. It's hard to go against the crowd; I've never been good at it.'

'What about loyalty or self-respect?'

Ruth swallowed hard but still couldn't speak. Her face was a splinter of ivory, eyes wide with shock.

'You'd better watch Debbie Pascoe,' warned Ben. 'It's a dangerous pleasure being her flavour of the day; you end up as tomorrow's leftovers.'

'I know. She wants to control everyone, and she's so vicious – Ben, what's the matter? Don't look at me like that.'

'You're amazing. When you're with her, you're running me down and now you're stabbing her in the back.'

'But – I thought you didn't like her?'

'The point is, she knows I don't like her. But you –'

'It's not like that. It's just – Debbie grinds people down. She can make life hell.'

'That's how bullies have power, because of people like you. Do you think Hitler could've built his gas chambers if it weren't for a whole bunch of Ruths running around, not wanting to go against the crowd?'

Ruth turned for home. She had nearly reached the crossroads when Ben stepped in front of her, blurred by a film of tears.

'Sorry,' he said, in a flat voice. 'I always expect too much of people, or so I've been told. The bus we want'll be here in five minutes – bus-stop's just over there.

The bus dropped them on the quayside of a small fishing village. The tide was out and the skeletons of small boats lay half buried in the mud, their stark ribs

51

pointing to the sky. Ruth wrinkled her nose at the strong, metallic smell of seaweed and rotting fish. Out across the harbour, larger boats bobbed in unison, glittering with bright paint and polished brass. Rigging jangled and flounced in the breeze and high above wheeled the seagull patrols.

'Come on,' said Ben. 'We've got some walking to do. There's a stone circle up on the moor that not many people know about. Sandwiches and coffee in here,' he added, waving his rucksack.

'What happens when we get there?'

'You have a look around, see what you can feel, whether you can recognise anything.'

Ruth swallowed, torn between feeling foolish and frightened.

'And what if this is where I find the – what we're looking for?'

'We get out as fast as we can.'

'In the dreams, it seems they can't do much yet; that thing they're calling on isn't strong enough.'

'Could well be. Anyway, it's a fine, sunny day.'

Ben was right. Evil belonged to the dark. 'Let's go then,' said Ruth.

They headed inland between tall hedgerows where the musty smell of warm grasses hung in the air and bluebottles blundered in drowsy circles. The road began to rise steeply, became a track edged by dry-stone walls, then a footpath. Behind them a sweep of land rushed down to the sea. Long grasses bent and rose with the wind in rhythmic waves and even the sturdiest farm buildings were far below. When they reached the top, they pushed on through heather and gorse into a world of wind and space and deep-blue sky. Then Ben stopped.

'There it is,' he breathed. It was a proud, perfect stone circle. Nineteen silvery pillars stood bright in the sunshine; a bracelet of stillness.

Ruth clenched her fists and walked straight into the centre. She turned slowly, listening, then moved up close to one of the stones. The erosion of tremendous age showed on its hollowed surface. The rock was wrapped in silvery green lichen and its face felt dry and rough. There was warmth from the sun and a steady pulse that might have been her own. Breaking contact, Ruth waved to Ben and collapsed into the heather. 'This isn't the place,' she said. 'What made you think it might be?'

Ben stretched out beside her, linking his hands behind his head. His sweatshirt rode up to reveal smooth brown skin. Ruth blushed and looked away, concentrating on what he was saying.

'It was what you said about the creatures bending the power their way to cause a disaster. These places are meant to hold the old power, the earth magic. It's a force without sides – could be used for good or bad. The stones are supposed to have healing powers and sometimes there's a skull or a few human bones buried in the centre, just about where you're sitting.'

Ruth flinched but forced her legs to stay still while Ben surveyed her with a vindictive grin on his face.

'Precision-built, this thing, you know,' he continued. 'But it was built thousands of years ago, when most people think men were hairy apes with clubs instead of brains.'

'What's new?' muttered Ruth.

'They reckon you can predict eclipses and the movement of the stars – Sorry, what did you say?'

'Nothing much. How do you know all this?'

'I'm interested, so I found out for myself. It's not the sort of thing they teach at school, but the local library's not bad.'

'Is that why you left school?'

Ben sat up, glaring. 'Wouldn't they all like to know that.'

'Oh, but I wouldn't tell them. I wouldn't say anything. Not now.'

Ben was silent.

'Anyway, forget it. I didn't mean to pry.'

'All right,' said Ben, slowly. 'I will tell you.'

'No, Ben, it doesn't ma—'

'Yes. Sign of faith, if you like. It was my dad. He always said I had to leave school as soon as it was legal, to work on the farm. I started studying for the exams, anyway. Thought I might be able to argue my way out of it, but he's not the type you can argue with. My mother wouldn't say anything – I can't ever remember her standing up for me, not against him.

'So, as soon as I turned fifteen, he was on to me. Said he wouldn't feed a man who couldn't earn his keep. I was what they call an Easter leaver. No qualifications.'

'But that's terrible! Couldn't the teachers do anything?'

'I told them I wanted to leave. I wasn't about to have my business all over the school. I think some of them even believed me. A few were just glad to see me go.'

'Why?'

'Well, I didn't make their classes very easy. "Has an enquiring mind" is how they used to put it on the reports.' Ben's smile was bitter. 'He didn't win, though. He lost his farm-hand the day after the end of term.'

'I didn't realise.'

'No need to feel sorry for me. I've got a job, haven't I? And I like it, working on cars. Sometimes, when I'm working on an engine, I'm thinking about how much more money I could make in one of the big cities. I could get away from slobs like that lot at your school. And all the gossips.'

'So why don't you?'

'I can't leave Cornwall. It drives me mad watching us sell mysteries to the tourists; flogging old Arthur. But it's not all cheap and sly and stupid. I can spend all day on metal and logical problems, then I come to a place like this and the whole thing changes. Cornwall really does have something, you see, once you get past all the trash. It belongs to the past: you're always aware of the old things.' Ben glanced sideways at her. 'Don't know why I'm telling you all this.'

'I'm glad you are. I was just thinking of all those people in the village who never hear you put more than two words together.'

'Yes, well, I'm not very good on scandal and the weather. Come on, let's have some of these sandwiches, that'll shut me up.'

That evening, Ruth crept in through the back door in case her mother was asleep. The house was still and light seeped from the sitting room. Easing the door open, Ruth saw her mother kneeling on the floor in front of the fire. The photograph album was open next to her. She was rocking and chanting, 'Brian, Brian, Brian,' in a hoarse whisper. Tears trickled down her cheeks.

Out in the back yard again, Ruth bit her knuckles hard, staring at nothing. Then she made a second, noisy entrance to the kitchen. 'I'm home, Mum,' she called. 'I'll make a cup of tea and bring it through, shall I?' Ruth's hand shook as she measured out the sugar, but five minutes later she was smiling as she carried in the tray.

Chapter Four

'Hello,' called Ruth, braking to a halt outside the garage. Ben nodded. He stood as though he was planted, dark and solid.

'Nasty drizzle, isn't it?'

'It's October,' explained Ben, frowning.

'Ah, yes, I remember – scandal and the weather.'

Ben looked at her in surprise, then he smiled and the stiffness went out of his shoulders. 'How was your week?'

'Two dreams –'

'I know; Tuesday and last night. Anything more to go on?'

'No. It just gets nearer and stronger every time. Like being in a maths exam with a problem I can't solve and only five minutes to go.' She tried to laugh but it came out as a wail. Ben took a step forward, then veered off to his bike and bent to check the front tyre. It was an old, heavy-framed machine, with a cracked leather saddle and no gears. Ruth suddenly wished her racer had less red paint and shiny chrome. She swallowed twice and found she could talk again.

'So – where to this week?'

'To the Men an Tol,' said Ben, straightening up.

'The what?'

'It means holed stone. If you pass a baby through the hole nine times, it's meant to be protected against illness. People still do it, so I thought the magic might be strong there. We have to go up the coast instead of down this time. Ready?'

The bike seemed to suit Ben. It was sturdy and held the road well. When they left the coast and began the climb to the moor, he stood on the pedals and just kept pushing until he reached the top. Ruth followed, watching the grey sweep of road hissing past under her wheels. Her knees were cold in her damp jeans and an irritable wind began to spit in her face. Once a cow sneezed at her over a wall, but they met nothing else and the sky grew steadily darker.

At last Ben stopped where a stony track forked off from the road. They left the bikes and squelched on through mud, slipping on rain-wet stones. Soon the road was out of sight and clouds, dark as bruises, were boiling over the skyline. Thunder muttered in the distance.

'Ben . . . do you think we'll be all right up here?'

'I don't know.'

'It's getting so dark. Suppose they're stronger when it's dark? I . . . I mean –'

'Will you stop acting as though I've got all the answers? For all I know, this is a trap and they're laughing at us now. But I'd rather be doing something, even if it's wrong. Do you want to sit at home and wait for it to happen?'

'No. I was just . . . trying to think ahead.'

'There's no point.'

Ruth fell silent. She thought perhaps there was a point, but Ben sounded so sure. They pressed on until they came to a wooden signpost and a footpath that went swimming through the grass. Ben looked at the sky. There was a flicker of something behind a cloud. The rain became insistent.

'Let's keep going,' he decided. 'We're nearly there.'

'Oh,' said Ruth, as they topped a small rise. 'Is that it? It just looks like a big Polo mint.'

The Men an Tol rested in a small hollow, guarded by two standing stones each as tall as Ruth was. She edged closer and touched the worn granite.

'Well, there's that pulsing again. But not disturbed, like in the dreams . . .'

Ben shifted uneasily, looking at the sky and the expanse of moor behind him. Ruth placed her palm on the rough, wet surface once again and concentrated.

'No,' she sighed. 'There's nothing here. I don't know, though –' She glanced about her. One ruined engine house brooded on the horizon, its gaunt tower seeming to support the weight of the storm clouds. 'Let's get back to the road.'

Ben shivered and turned up the collar of his coat. 'Perhaps it's just the storm.'

Ruth said nothing, but her eyes were huge, unblinking.

'OK,' agreed Ben. 'Back to the road.'

They set off, two dots of colour swamped in a grey tide of cloud and moor. Each step they took came more quickly than the last, but not once did they look behind them.

The storm broke as they were riding back. Huge drops of rain hit the road with such force, they bounced inches in the air.

'Bus shelter – two minutes,' yelled Ben.

It was a sturdy stone building with a low, wooden bench inside. Ruth sat watching the road become a lake and wished she was curled up in a warm bed. 'What good are we doing? We're running round in circles and it just gets nearer.'

'But we're closer already, Ruth. We can cross two places off the list now. We'll find it as long as we keep going.' Ben nodded encouragement, sending droplets of water flying from his hair.

'What then?' she asked. They stared at each other until her eyes ached with the desire to cry and she turned away, biting her lip.

'Food,' said Ben, opening his saddle-bag. 'That's what we need, and a hot drink.'

'You sound just like my dad. He thought the answer to everything was a cup of tea . . .' Ruth tailed off and glared at the rain. Here it comes, she thought. Embarrassed silence. Change of subject.

'What was he like, then, your dad?'

'What was he like? Oh, well . . . You mean, what was he like?'

'Yes. Did he look like you?'

'He was skinny like me and his hair was thick, but it was a sort of sandy colour and he had blue eyes . . .'

'Did he have a job?'

'In a car factory; that's why they moved to Coventry in the first place. He hated it. He really wanted me to get on at school so I wouldn't be stuck like he was. Every night I had to tell him about the lessons and he'd want to see my work – oh, it drove me mad sometimes. He'd spend a fortune on collecting those educational magazine sets with special plastic folders to keep them in and I never used them.

He'd have a fit if he could see my marks now.'

'What else?'

'Well, he was in the factory darts team and he had a special jumper with the team crest on; he was ever so proud of it. He always washed it himself and mum would get all offended because she thought he didn't trust her with it. They really loved each other though. Dad never seemed to notice she was getting fat; he thought she was beautiful, hugging and kissing her all the time.'

Ruth talked on until the clouds paled and they were able to cycle home. She coasted to a halt at the village crossroads and Ben drew up beside her, his front wheel sending up a fountain of spray.

'Next Saturday?'

Ben nodded. 'Take care,' he said, and then ducked his head and turned towards the garage.

On Monday, Ruth opened the classroom door to a sudden silence. She turned round, expecting to find a teacher, but the doorway was empty.

'It's all right. They're all still in the staff meeting.'

Silence still gripped the room. Everyone was staring.

Ruth felt the sweat beginning to prickle under her arms.

'What's the matter?'

She looked for Debbie and found her perched on a desk. As soon as their eyes met, Debbie sent five words floating across the room. 'Prefer them rough, do you?'

'What do you mean?'

It was Alison who answered. 'We called in to see you on Saturday and your mum told us you were out

61

with Ben Treseder. So why have you been letting us think he was bothering you, and why did you tell us you had to work in the shop that day?'

Ruth thought of Saturday and the way Ben had listened to her. When she spoke, her voice was calm and strong. 'Sorry, Alison. I shouldn't've told you that. I'll be out with Ben most weekends from now on.'

Debbie frowned and her small, neat foot began to swing, the gold ankle chain reflecting the light with a fish-scale glitter. This was not working out like the last time.

'You mean you prefer Ben Treseder's company to ours?'

'Well, if you want to put it like that, yes.'

Debbie's soft, red mouth dropped open and one of the boys laughed, but Ruth didn't notice. Just for a moment a cage she had built inside herself crumbled and something was set free.

That's me, she thought, and smiled.

Debbie saw the smile and misunderstood. Her face turned mean and tight. 'I'll get you for this,' she hissed.

It started in the first lesson. Mr Pugh stood in a swirling mist of chalk dust, looking faintly fungoid in the pale sunlight. He was giving notes on the Tudors; Ruth watched him as he droned lists of facts into the heavy classroom air. His black hair was slicked back with oil and gleamed like a raven's back. His black suit was shiny with age. Although a bony, hunched little man, still all his clothes were too tight. His shirt collar bit into his neck and his black shoes were laced so firmly, they squealed when he walked.

Ten minutes from the end he unhooked his glasses

and massaged an angry red mark etched across the bridge of his nose. This was a sign they all knew; the notes were over. There were sighs of relief, pens clattered on to desks and the slow writers rubbed their cramped hands.

'Right,' he said, 'a bit of light relief. Turn to page twenty-nine of *Tudor Britain* and copy out either the knight in armour or the courtly lady. No felt-tips.' With muffled groans they settled down and Mr Pugh began to prowl the room.

No one seemed to know where the piece of paper came from; it was suddenly there, circling the desks and carrying with it an infectious, choking laugh. Mr Pugh stiffened, sniffing the air, then he homed in. The boy handed over the paper with sickening eagerness.

'It wasn't me, sir.'

The class was still, watching with horrified fascination to see what he would do next. His breath grew harsh and heavy as he stared at the paper. His head shot up and he glared, watching thirty faces fall before his eyes.

Mr Pugh began a slow walk down Ruth's aisle, his shoes squealing at every step. She waited, head down, for him to pass, but the squealing stopped. He brought his face down on a level with hers in a swift, bird-like movement. Startled, she looked into his eyes and thought of pickled eggs.

'Well, young lady?' he hissed, slamming the paper on to her desk. On it was drawn a wickedly funny caricature of Mr Pugh. He was clutching a piece of chalk and, on the blackboard behind him were the words, 'Keep Cornwall green, have sex with a frog'.

'I didn't draw that, sir.'

Mr Pugh brought his face closer and opened his mouth. He had too many teeth and a yellow nicotine smear on his upper lip.

'Let me see your book.'

Ruth handed over her unfinished notes with a sinking feeling. 'Sir, I didn't –'

'Li-ar! What were you doing when everyone else was taking notes? These are your initials at the bottom, aren't they? R.D.? Well?'

Ruth could think of nothing to say.

'I won't forget this, girl. Oh, no, I won't forget. See me after the lesson.'

Debbie smiled at the back of the class.

So it went on. Ruth came out of the shower after gym to find her towel and knickers lying in a pool of water. In cookery, a good handful of salt was added to her cake mixture. She sat alone in every lesson and never went near the toilets at break. Her one moment of sure strength was being eaten away by the steady, dripping poison of Debbie's campaign and Ruth lay awake for some time on Tuesday night, trying to recapture it. When she did sleep, she dreamed of walking across sand-dunes carrying a melting ice-cream cornet. She was trying to spot the person she had bought it for before it dripped away completely, when someone changed the channel . . .

She cowers in the darkness but they find her, drag her towards the growing noise. Pounding shakes the world. Frantically, she looks behind her, searching for escape. What she sees makes the breath catch in her throat. There are other people, all around.

'Oh, please, please help.'

She tries again, her voice rising. 'Please, over here. We must try to get out.'

Once again, screaming. 'Move! Everyone move!'

There is no response.

She becomes aware that the creatures are watching her, shaking with laughter. Their pale, slit eyes find hers and the voices start.

'They cannot see us.'

'They will not hear you.'

'They cannot sense the power.'

'They will all die.'

Ruth woke up wet with sweat. She began to cry on a high, hopeless note, clasping her knees and rocking back and forth. Madness did not feel far away.

At midday on Wednesday Ruth ran from the school to the garage through a steady downpour. The big double doors of the workshop were shut. She splashed through the oily puddles of the forecourt and peered through a gap in the panelling. Inside it was still and dark, the high roof lost in shadows. A light shone from the tiny office but the door was locked and a cardboard clock in the window was set to one-thirty. Ruth dashed round to the side of the building and up the iron staircase to Ben's flat. She hammered on the door for a full minute before slumping back against the guardrail. Then she pulled a note from her pocket, pushed it through the letterbox and began the walk back to school. She had missed lunch.

As the afternoon wore on, the teachers' voices grew small and far away in the stuffy classrooms. Ruth moved uncomfortably inside her damp clothes and shivered. By evening her cheeks were flushed and her eyes bright with fever. Her head felt like a huge balloon full of bees and she ached all over. She lay in bed, drifting in and out of sleep. Once she thought she saw her dad, standing by the bed. 'A little shop in Cornwall, that's what we'll have,' he promised, but when she looked again, the room was empty.

Then Ben came in, bringing all the people from her dream. He stared at her, his deep-blue eyes shining in the light from the bedside lamp. 'You're crazy,' he jeered, 'it's only a nightmare. Nothing's going to happen. All these people are sure of it.'

The dream people nodded, then started to laugh. They laughed and laughed and then her mother was there and the laughter was wind and rain battering the house. Downstairs, Rusty howled in lonely misery.

'That Ben Treseder keeps phoning,' said Mrs Davis on Friday. 'I told him you wouldn't be well enough to go tomorrow, not after that nasty flu.'

'Oh,' said Ruth, staring at the kitchen table.

'You – kept talking to him on Wednesday night – you know, when you had that really high temperature. You kept telling him how you hadn't let him down this time.'

'Did I?'

'Ruthie, don't let it get too serious; you're not old enough.'

Ruth, worn out and pinched-looking, said nothing.

A soft grey morning light was at the window when Ruth opened her eyes. Rain tapped against the pane, then stopped. She began to drift back to sleep. Again the spatter of rain, harder this time, then a steady plink, plink, plink and a skitter of pebbles down the sloping outside sill. When Ruth looked out, the view had disappeared, blotted out by thick fog, and Ben was standing in the yard, his arm pulled back for another throw. He dropped the pebbles, tapped his watch and beckoned impatiently.

Downstairs in the shadowy kitchen, Ruth edged around the table with Rusty snuffling at her heels.

'Come on,' whispered Ben when she opened the back door. 'We've got to get away before your mum wakes up.'

'But I haven't been well and, anyway, she'll wonder where I've gone.'

'Leave her a note.'

Rusty was quiet until Ruth eased shut the back door, then he whimpered. The whimper became a whine which began to build into a howl. Ruth gave a frantic glance at her mother's bedroom window.

'We'll have to take him with us,' she whispered.

Wordlessly, Ben turned and settled his bike against the yard wall.

They headed for the bus-stop through a muffling whiteness. The foghorn from the lighthouse called regularly, each deep bellow echoing from the cliffs.

'I got your note about the dream,' said Ben. 'They're getting confident, letting you see the others. Did you recognise anyone?'

'No, it wasn't clear enough for that. It was horrible, the way they all just stood there; worse than being alone. I think that's why I was allowed to see them.'

'Nice way to get their kicks,' muttered Ben.

'Where're we going today, anyway? Near the Men an Tol? Last Saturday, there was something –'

'Yes, that's what I thought. There's an old chambered tomb not far from there. Want to try it?'

Ruth studied Ben as they waited for the bus. All week she had held a picture of him in her mind, but the picture had been smiling, not scowling with eyes still swollen from sleep. Surely he had been taller and hadn't the hair been less . . . the clothes more . . . ?

But wait till he hears how I stuck up for him at school. Then he'll smile.

The bus moved slowly, with fog swirling in its headlights like the cold breath of the sea. Ruth watched white houses glide, ghost-like, past the window while she put together words that would tell what she had been through without sounding boastful.

'They found out, last week, that I was still seeing you.'

'Who did?'

'That lot at school.'

Ben turned sharply in his seat. 'You mean you hadn't told them?'

Ruth blinked, then tried again. 'I stuck up for you this time, Ben. None of them are talking to me now . . .'

Ben did smile then, but it was cold and bitter. 'Some people have all the luck,' he said.

Ruth swallowed the rest of her story and stared at her clenched fists instead.

The bus had turned inland and passed the track to the Men an Tol before Ben swayed to the front.

'You take care, now, in that fog,' said the driver before he opened the doors. They stepped off on to a well-kept grass verge and watched the winking tail-lights of the bus until they disappeared.

'This way,' said Ben, and leapt over a stile that breached the dry-stone wall behind them.

'Go on, boy, up you get.' Ruth patted the top of the stile. Rusty danced on his toes, whining, until she clasped her hands under his rump and boosted him up. She climbed after him and stayed there for a few seconds, looking around. She saw a field of bumps and hollows, covered by coarse grass. Standing ahead of her, twined in coils of fog, was a huge three-legged footstool. It was tall enough for Ben to stand, stooped, under the horizontal slab.

Ruth grabbed Rusty's lead and stalked across the field. 'I thought you said it was a tomb,' she snapped.

Ben gestured around the field. 'Underneath,' he said, 'it's full of early Britons.'

'So where's the entrance?'

'We can't get into it; we don't really need to.' He patted the silvery grey stone. 'This is a dolmen. Most people call them table stones now –'

'Then why don't you?'

Ben looked at her but said nothing. Turning away, Ruth moved up to the stone, leaned against it and tried to concentrate.

'Well?' said Ben.

'Well what? Stop treating me like a performing seal.'

'Honk, honk,' said Ben. 'Try again.'

'No.'

'Why not?'

'Shut up.'

Ben surveyed her coolly. 'Try it.'

'Leave me alone, you Cornish idiot! So much for your precious research. Are you sure you're using the books properly? Know what an index is, do you?'

'Ruth, stop it – please,' pleaded Ben, his voice tight and quiet as though he had locked it away. But Ruth could not stop.

'Perhaps you'd do better with picture books. Come on, lost your tongue? I mean, I know you don't have a very big vocabulary, but –'

Ben snapped. She saw it happen. His face was the same but whatever made his ordinary looks so attractive was gone. 'You're just like that lot at school,' he hissed. 'Knowledge but no sense. You're right; I am stupid, because I thought you were different. I thought we –

'Well, I've had enough of this. I can think of better things to do with my Saturdays than standing in foggy fields letting half-witted kids take out their frustrations on me. I think I'll go home and work on my phonetic spelling. I'm already on to the green book.'

She let him go without protest and leaned back against the rough stone.

A far-away yelp came out of the fog.

'Rusty?' The puppy was nowhere in sight. 'Rusty!'

Nothing.

Oh no. Oh God. Please.

'Come on, Rusty. Here, boy!' Ruth began to stumble across the field, her eyes bandaged by the fog.

'Rusty! Rusty! Rusty!'

'I think it came from over there,' said Ben behind her.

'Oh, Ben, I must've dropped his lead when we were –'

'Shhh.'

A faint whimper seeped out of the fog. They ran until they came to a stream swollen by days of rain. It flowed fast and silent and the banks were steep.

'Do you think . . . ?'

They ran and stopped and ran again, scanning the water.

'There!' yelled Ruth, pointing towards a stone near the middle of the stream. Rusty was scrabbling frantically for a hold on it but his lead was tangled in bushes on the bank. Every time he lunged for the stone, his collar choked him and he went under. He was tiring fast.

'Rusty!' shouted Ben. 'Why doesn't he just turn back?'

Ruth pulled off her boots and plunged in, gasping. She snapped the tough, whippy twigs that held the puppy's lead and began to pull him towards her. He went under. Ben jumped in, lifted him out and threw him up on to the bank. Rusty coughed a few times, then stood up, quivering. He looked thin and cold, with his coat plastered against his ribs. Ruth's jeans were wet to the thigh and Ben's sweater sagged with the weight of water it carried.

'How come we get soaked even when it's not raining?' he asked.

Then Rusty shook himself. Spray flew everywhere and the look on Ben's face made Ruth giggle. Ben looked at her and began to splutter. They laughed until they collapsed on to the grass. Ben clutched Ruth's arm and shook his head at her to stop but every time their eyes met it started again. Rusty tried to lick some sense into them but it only made things worse.

'Oh . . . oh . . . stop,' croaked Ruth, flapping her hands weakly, 'before I wet myself.' Then they both looked down at her soaking jeans.

'How will we tell?' asked Ben, and they were off again.

Finally, when she was too tired to laugh any more, Ruth picked herself up and tried to force her wet feet back into her boots.

'Ben, about what I said: I didn't mean it. It's just that I've had such a bad week . . .'

'I know. My fault for not understanding. It must be difficult when you're not used to being on the outside.'

Ruth stood up and nearly sat down again. 'I feel a bit odd; like I'm floating.'

'We'd better get home,' said Ben. 'It's my stupid fault for dragging you out here.' He looked so anxious that she stepped forward and kissed him. His lips were warm and soft.

'Thanks for coming back.'

'And thank you,' said Ben. 'I could just do with a nice flu bug.' But his eyes were gentle when he looked at her, the pupils wide and dark.

Chapter Five

It was Wednesday before Ruth felt strong enough for school and Debbie. She left home early and stopped at the garage gates in the hope of seeing Ben. He came out immediately, smiling and smoothing down the front of his oil-smeared boilersuit.

'I've been watching for you. You look better than you did. How's Rusty? Was your mam very angry?'

'He's fine and she didn't even notice. She hardly notices anything these days.'

'But what about your note? And I left my bike in the yard.'

'Probably got up and went straight into the shop. She must've missed breakfast.'

But she didn't miss me. Ruth pushed the thought away and added, 'So, that was a bit of luck, wasn't it?'

Ben looked at her closely, then reached forward and softly touched her cheek with the back of his hand.

'Listen, what are you doing next week?' he asked.

'What do you mean?'

'It's your half-term.'

Ruth blinked with shock. 'I didn't realise. I've been here seven weeks then. Seems like for ever.'

'I know; it's been tough. Listen, Ruth –' said Ben, and stopped, scowling at his boots.

'I'm listening.'

'What about Bodmin Moor?'

'Bodmin Moor?' echoed Ruth.

'Yes. Loads of possible sites there – you should look at the map. I think it's time we went further; we're not having much luck here, are we?'

'You mean, we should go there?'

'Yes.' The scowl deepened.

'For the week? But – I don't know whether Mum'd let me. I mean – where would we stay?'

'With Rosemary and Jack, my aunt and uncle. Look, if you don't want to go, just say so, will you? I've got a lot of work –'

'Yes. Yes, I'd like to go, really. Really, Ben.'

Ben finally looked up, his shoulders relaxed and he let out a great breath of air. 'Right,' he said, and grinned.

'Bodmin Moor? With Ben Treseder?' Mrs Davis stopped in her tracks, tea-towel in one hand, dripping plate in the other.

'With his aunt and uncle,' said Ruth hastily.

'Who are they?'

'Jack and – I mean, Mr and Mrs Penfold. They sound very nice. I've got the phone number here.' Ruth dried her hands and fished a scrap of paper from the back pocket of her jeans. 'She's expecting you to phone and sort things out. Shall I finish that?'

Mrs Davis looked down at her hands, put down the plate and tea-towel and took the paper. She stared at the number with a puzzled frown as though it was in code. Then she gave a slight shake of the head and patted her hair into place.

'Penfold,' she tried, and walked out of the kitchen, closing the door behind her.

Ruth stood still, her head full of prepared answers that had not been needed. Then she left the dishes and crept through to the living room. With her ear pressed to the door she could hear her mother in the hall, dialling the number.

'Hello, is that Mrs Penfold? . . . This is Mrs Davis, Ruth's mum. It's very kind of you to offer to look after her for the week, but are you sure . . . ?'

Ruth held her breath still in her throat and crossed her fingers.

'I see. Have you got enough room . . . ? Oh, a room of her own . . . Yes, I'm sure she will. Well, I must say I'm very grateful . . . No, really . . .'

Ruth whirled from the door and danced across the room to Rusty. She had heard enough.

'We're going, Rusty, we're going,' she whispered in his silky ear.

'There it is,' sang Rosemary Penfold, pointing a skinny arm across the slow rise and fall of the moor to a white farmhouse. 'And there's Jack!'

She brought the Land Rover to a screeching halt and slammed the palm of her hand on to the horn. A distant figure in the yard looked up and waved.

Ben was excited, leaning forward in his seat. 'See that long, low building across the yard from the house? That's the boarding kennels. And there's the barn; I used to camp in that when I was little. And that walled-in bit, over on the south side of the house, that's Jack's vegetable garden, and –'

But Ben had time for no more because Rosemary had put her foot down. Rusty shot back under the seat, where he had spent most of the journey. Ruth, who had been feeling lighter with every mile from the village, threw back her head in the blustery sunshine and laughed.

Jack Penfold was Ben twenty years on. The thick, dark hair was cut severely short with a peppering of grey and the broad features were heavier, blurred by time. Ruth stared, and did not feel rude about doing so because Jack's blue eyes were fixed on Rosemary. As she stepped from the driving seat, he caught her up in a hug and pushed his face into her dark-blonde hair.

That evening they ate in the big kitchen while Rusty dozed in front of the fire and the wind howled at the windows. Rosemary lit candles even though everyone was in jeans and none of the crockery matched.

'I love their light,' she said, her bony hands arched above the flame.

Jack had made a fish pie with light, golden pastry and he served it with creamy potatoes, broccoli and buttered carrots fresh from the garden.

'It's delicious,' said Ruth and he beamed, looking at her properly for the first time.

'Let's have some wine,' cried Rosemary. 'I've got some three-year-old apple you must try, Ruth.'

Suddenly it was an occasion. Jack brought on homemade bread, a bowl of fruit and some cheese, and the hours flowed by. At first Rosemary carried the conversation, pushing back the sleeves of her jumper and throwing her heavy plait of hair over one shoulder as she talked. Her great brown eyes glowed and her mouth curved in a smile that was impossible

76

to resist. Soon even Jack was talking, telling Ruth about his vegetable garden.

'Two enemies we've got up here – the wind and the animals. That's why it's walled, you see. Mrs Toms, up along the moor a bit, she had some tourists come to buy eggs and they left her gate open. Half her vegetables went to the ponies and the sheep before she realised.'

'Bloody tourists,' snapped Ben and Ruth jumped in her seat. 'They come here and muck us about for half the year, blocking up the roads. They push the prices of the cottages sky high so none of the locals can afford them. Bloody menaces.'

Ruth was shocked at the way his temper had come barging into the peaceful kitchen. She glanced sideways at Rosemary who, quite deliberately, winked.

'Now, Ben,' she said, her eyes sparkling, 'you know they just about keep Cornwall going. I mean, fishing's not so good since the pilchards stopped coming and as for the tin mines . . . All we've got is farming and the tourists.'

'Yes, but they bring nothing but exhaust fumes. What about bringing us some investment for industry? And don't say we're too far from London. Who needs motorways, anyway; there's the sea routes – direct exporting to the continent . . .'

'You're talking like a Cornish Nationalist,' laughed Rosemary.

Ruth watched Ben's face darken. He leaned across the table, took a deep breath –

'Cornish Nationalists?' she blurted. 'But this isn't a country. You're English.'

Ben made a sound like a pressure cooker letting off steam, but Rosemary ignored him. 'I think Corn-

wall's always been different, stuck out here surrounded by sea,' she said. 'The people feel – separate.
We even had our own Celtic language, but that's dead
now.'

'It's not! What about when they light the mid-
summer's night bonfire at St Just? Some of the
ceremony's in English but there's a lot in old
Cornish.'

'And can you understand it, Ben?'

Ben scowled and began ripping the peel from an
orange.

'Anyway,' continued Rosemary, unabashed,
'what's this nationalism, except an excuse for wars?'

'People need something to be proud of.'

'Pride? That's a man's word if ever I heard one.'

'So you'd want everyone to be the same all over the
country? Because that's what would happen if people
weren't proud of things. You'd lose saffron cake and
pasties and furry dances and Cornish wrestling and
kiddley broth and hurling and –'

'OK, Ben.'

'– Cousin Jacks and clotted cream and –'

'OK, Ben. Point taken. Let's hear what Ruth
thinks for a change.'

'I sort of know what you mean – about the people
being separate. They're not exactly unfriendly, but
my mum never gets past the how are yous and chats
about the weather. She keeps saying call me Eileen,
but it's always Mrs Davis.'

'I remember,' said Jack, 'in my village there was a
family whose grandparents came from Dorset. They
were still called the incomers three generations
later.'

'That's another thing I've noticed; time seems

different here. It's all more – permanent and . . . this'll sound stupid . . .'

'No, go on, Ruth.'

'Well. You've all got telephones and televisions and freezers and – and everything that goes with modern life, but –' Ruth broke off and stared into the candle flame. 'But it's just a skin and there's something older and harder hiding underneath. Like topsoil over granite. But sometimes the granite pokes through.'

Jack was watching her closely. 'When have you seen the granite?'

Ruth glanced at Ben, who gave the slightest shake of his head. 'Oh, I don't know,' she said, 'all the stone circles and so on – and Ben was telling me about the old legends.'

'Ah, now, if you're interested in the old stories, then you've come to the right place. Jack's an expert, aren't you, love?'

Jack was still staring at Ruth and took a few seconds to answer. 'What? Well, I know a few. Want to hear some?'

Jack told a story like a carver working a piece of wood. With swift, spare strokes he followed the twists and curves of the plot, never going against the grain. He polished up each scene until it glowed like oiled wood and he always knew when the shape was complete.

Finally, he pushed his chair back from the table and broke the spell. 'Eleven o'clock, Rosie. Shall I help you check the kennels?'

'Oh, you wicked man. Any excuse to get me alone with all that clean straw and soft lighting. Come on, I'll race you.'

They fell out of the door, giggling, leaving Ben and Ruth alone with a pile of dirty dishes.

'The demon drink,' sighed Ben, shaking his head.

'Oh, but isn't Rosemary great?' said Ruth, loading the sink. 'I can't believe she's only a couple of years younger than my mum. She doesn't dress her age, does she? Do you get on well, usually?'

'What do you mean, usually?'

'Well, you got a bit angry tonight.'

'No, she just enjoys getting me going – it's not serious. Even if it was, it's not always a bad thing to get angry, you know.'

'It always has been in my house. As long as things are nice and smooth on the surface, my mum's happy, no matter what's festering underneath. I think that's why I have to get really angry before I can say anything and then it's always too much. I'm working on it, though, Ben – saying what I think – I really am. Do you always say what you're thinking?'

'Yes,' said Ben. 'Give us a kiss.'

Ruth woke up to a Sunday sullen with rain, but the smell of fresh-baked bread was drifting up the stairs and she had not dreamed. In the kitchen, Rusty was snoring and Jack was taking the last of a batch of loaves from the oven. He ducked his head shyly as he said good morning; the Jack of wine and stories was gone.

Ben was at the table, eating a thick slice of bread and honey. His hair was sticking up and he needed a shave.

'You look like Desperate Dan,' said Ruth, settling opposite him. There was a choked splutter from Jack's corner of the kitchen.

'And there was I thinking I looked very sexy,' said Ben, pretending to be offended.

'Where's Rosemary?'

'She's been out in the kennels for the last hour,' said Ben, pouring her a cup of tea. Ruth watched, savouring the strangeness of sharing breakfast with him. 'We'll go out and help her when you've had something to eat. No point in going out on the moor in weather like this.'

Outside, they scurried across the muddy farmyard while the wind tried to throw handfuls of water down their necks. The moor was hidden by grey muslin screens of rain. A dusty stillness and the sweet smell of fresh straw settled around them as they closed the shed door.

'Morning,' called Rosemary. 'I've saved a good job for you two. There's a litter in that far stall. Their bitch died so they have to be bottle-fed. Here you are.' She handed Ruth a pail of warm water with five feeding bottles bobbing in it.

The puppies were in a pile on a bed of straw. They were tiny and very short-sighted but they all began to wobble towards Ruth, mewling from mouths as pink as cherry blossom.

'Look at that,' said Ben. 'They can hear the clink of a bottle in a pail at fifty paces.'

Ruth reached for the nearest puppy. It fitted neatly into one hand, its round belly supported in her palm. She could feel its heart pulsing against the delicate wall of its chest as it snuffled and sighed, pulling strongly at the bottle teat.

With a delighted smile, Ruth looked up at Ben. He grinned back, then leaned forward, bringing his face close enough for her to smell the breakfast honey on his breath. They kissed, bumped noses, tried again. Their hands were full of puppies and feeding bottles but they edged round until they were sitting side by side, pressed together.

The puppy Ruth was feeding let go of the teat, burped and fell into a deep sleep. She laid it in the straw, scooped up the next one and settled herself comfortably against Ben's shoulder.

'This,' sighed Ben, leaning his head against the wooden stall divider, 'is perfect.'

The day passed, framed by the routines of work and Jack's cooking. There were three cold, wet trips to the back field to exercise Rusty and the boarding dogs and they spent hours in the musky warmth of the shed with the rain drilling on the corrugated tin roof. By the time night draped itself across the moor, their search had turned into a holiday without either of them realising it.

Monday was blown in on a strong wind but the sky was cold and clear. 'Time to start looking,' said Ruth, and felt no fear at the thought.

'What about Hensbarrow Downs?' asked Ben, pointing to a spot on the map he had spread on the kitchen table. Ruth saw the symbol for a beacon marking the highest part of the downs and next to it was written, 'prehistoric barrows'.

'What are they?'

'Communal burial chambers.'

'OK,' she said, 'let's give it a try.'

Out on the moor the wind had a free run across miles of empty land before it hit them with the bullying force of a rugby scrum. Ruth, struggling over the rough ground, felt like a snail trying to cross a football pitch, but when she looked back after half an hour, there was no sign of the road or the farmhouse.

'You'd be surprised how many get lost within half a mile of the road,' said Ben. 'Especially when the fog comes down.'

'At least I can let Rusty off the lead now.'

Ben shook his head. 'I wouldn't do that,' he said. 'Look over there.' Ruth followed his pointing finger to an unexpected clump of wild moorland ponies. Tough, hairy little creatures, they grazed with a concentrated determination, clamping their long, yellow teeth on to the grass as though to stop the wind from gusting it away.

'And over there,' Ben added.

Ruth frowned, bewildered. 'What?'

'That lovely patch of soft green grass. Looks inviting, doesn't it? Try to walk on that and you could sink without trace – it's a bog. Probably a few sheep and ponies under there.'

Ruth stared at the bright surface with its hidden horrors underneath and shivered. She was glad when it was no longer in sight.

They reached the beacon at about midday. The barrows were nothing more than soft mounds under the topsoil, like the upturned hulls of long-forgotten boats. Ruth moved up close, shutting out the bright autumn day and feeling for the menace of her dreams.

She shrugged. 'It's about as menacing as a pair of slippers. In fact, since we came to Bodmin, the whole thing feels unreal, like we were playing a game.'

'Have we moved out of their reach, do you think?'

'Perhaps. . . .'

'Oh, hell, I don't know. Let's find somewhere out

of this wind to eat. You can let Rusty go now, if you like; there won't be any bogs on this higher ground.'

Ben was quiet throughout the meal and, afterwards, he spent a long time packing everything away and fussing with the straps of his rucksack.

'Ruth –' he began, still tugging at a strap already fastened, 'suppose, just suppose, the dreams stopped and there was nothing to solve – would you still want to see me? Because your dreams aren't the only reason I wanted to bring you here. I wanted you to see the moor and meet Rosemary and Jack . . . I wanted to spend some time with you away from that damned village – I –'

'Yes, I would,' said Ruth and she leaned across and kissed him gently on the ear, running a finger along the line of his jaw. He turned and saw her green eyes shining.

'Ruth,' he breathed, and his voice quivered. 'I love you.'

They kissed and Ruth pushed a hand under the fleecy warmth of his sweatshirt, feeling the curve of his spine under smooth skin. His arms came around her and they cradled down together on the cold ground.

The excitement that bloomed inside her was a new sensation. Back in Coventry, when Steven Friars had taken her to the cinema, she had felt nothing but irritation when he started squeezing her thigh and fumbling with her clothes instead of watching the film. And when, after a school disco, John Wallace kissed her and stuck his tongue in her mouth, all she had felt was sick. But they had been more like skirmishes in a war than acts of love; surprise attacks with her forced into the role of defender.

Ben tangled his legs with hers and pulled her close for a second kiss. Then Rusty tumbled down into the hollow. He trampled all over them, snuffling and yelping, planting his cold nose and wet tongue wherever he found bare skin.

'My God!' yelled Ben, jumping to his feet. 'It's the vice squad!'

'I'm sorry, Ben,' said Ruth, struggling to get Rusty's lead attached to his collar. 'He thought it was a game.'

Ben gave a rueful smile. 'Probably just as well he arrived. We were getting a bit carried away, there.'

'Yes,' muttered Ruth, straightening her clothes, 'we were.' She bit her lip.

'Hey, don't worry. It's OK. Nothing's going to happen until we're both good and ready. In fact, let's just get used to being a – what do they say in those American films? An item.'

Ruth smiled. 'All right. You know,' she added, slipping her arms around his waist, 'in those films, the boy always gives the girl something of his to wear, like . . . a sweatshirt.'

'A sort of announcement? Good idea. You can have my grey socks. Ow! All right, all right, my lime-green Y-fronts. Ouch! OK, I give in.' Ben stepped back and began to drag his sweatshirt over his head.

'Not now, idiot,' giggled Ruth, pulling it down again. Then she grabbed his hands and looked up into his face. 'Ben? I love you too.'

The next day Ruth found Rosemary in front of the kitchen fire. She had just washed her hair and was combing the whole heavy length of it forward from the nape of her neck to hang over her face. Lifting her head, she parted the blonde curtain briefly. 'There's tea in the pot. Excuse me while I dry this haystack. It always takes ages.'

Rosemary bent forward again and went back to combing while Ruth settled into the armchair opposite.

'Having a good time?'

'Great, thanks.'

'Ben's really taken to you, hasn't he? It's not often he'll risk getting close; most people find him, well, surly.'

'Yes, I was scared of him to start with – he seemed to be in a constant bad mood. He's different when you get to know him.'

'It's what he had to put up with at home, you see.'

'You mean about his dad making him leave school? That's why he left the farm, wasn't it?'

Rosemary's surprised face peered out from behind her hair. 'He told you? Well, he really has taken to you. I knew you must be something special when he asked to bring you up here. He's never done that before.'

'He really loves it here,' said Ruth. 'He's a different person.'

'That's funny, he said exactly the same thing about you. When he still lived at home, he used to come up here nearly every holiday. We loved having him and it meant he could get away from his dad for a while. Oh, the rows I've had with that man! I call him the black hole. You know, those gaps in space full of negative energy, or something? He sucks all the energy and pleasure out of anyone around him. Now Ben's mum is Jack's sister and they've got the same sensitive nature. It doesn't take much to knock the stuffing out of them and she's had years of it, poor girl.

'Ben understood, I think, about her not standing up to his dad over the school. What knocked him for six was that she never tried to get in touch with him after he left, except for one note asking him not to send any more letters in case his dad found out.'

'But – she could've written to him without his dad knowing, or visited, even.'

'I know.' Rosemary flung back her hair and sat up. 'So, you see, if he's put his trust in someone, it's important they don't let him down. He might not be able to take it.'

Ruth winced. The memory of her disloyalty and the fight was like a stinging nettle. Rosemary was watching her, waiting for an answer, so she began to talk.

'The girls at school don't like him, but then they're not very good judges. There's this creep called Ian Ryder and they all think he's great and their parents see him as a good catch because his parents own a big market garden. I don't know, I suppose he's good-looking, wears nice clothes, but at the school disco, he practically raped me right in the middle of the hall.'

Rosemary grimaced. 'Charming. I seem to remember his dad being just the same.'

'They can't see how nasty he is – all surface charm and slimy underneath, like those bogs up on the moor. Ben, he's much more – well, just much more. I wouldn't hurt him now, not if I could help it.'

Rosemary gave her a smile full of warmth. 'No wonder he likes you. You can see more than most.'

Even in my dreams, thought Ruth, but she could

not stop a growing hope that the nightmares were over. And every night, for the rest of that week, her sleep was deep and untroubled.

Ruth opened the back gate on Sunday with her head still full of the high moors and homemade wine in the firelight.

'I'm home, Mum,' she called, backing into the kitchen with her arms loaded. Her mother stood passively for a kiss on the cheek, pale and plump and faded. Ruth felt someone tie a knot in her shoulder muscles but she kept on smiling.

'Rusty's grown, hasn't he? He ran for miles across the moors. Jack sent these,' she added, putting a bag of eggs and a huge fruit cake on the kitchen table. 'He's a wonderful cook. Do you want to try some of that cake now, with a cup of tea?'

She waited while Mrs Davis seemed to come back from a long way away. 'Yes. Yes, I'll put the kettle on. Ruthie – it's nice to have you home again.'

Her bedroom was silent and cold, with an impersonal tidiness that made Ruth think of hotels. She began to whistle loudly as she emptied her bag and took her dirty washing into the echoing bathroom. Turning from the laundry basket, she was about to put her toothbrush in the glass when her hand froze and her breath stopped in mid-whistle. She was motionless for a second, arm out in front of her, lips pursed. Then her eyes widened and her arm began to tremble. The toothbrush clattered to the floor, her breath came back in a harsh gasp and she whirled around. Again she stopped, staring at the bathroom door, before breaking into a stumbling run.

'Good timing. Tea's ready,' said Mrs Davis.

'Mum – in the bathroom –' Ruth swallowed and tried again. 'Mum – Dad's shaving things, they're set out in the bathroom – and his dressing gown – behind the door . . .'

Her voice faltered as she spotted her father's overcoat hanging next to her school blazer. Wordless, she turned back to her mother, but Mrs Davis refused to meet her eyes.

'I – put them there,' she whispered.

'You put – but why? Do you know what it did to me?'

'I'm sorry, Ruthie. I meant to move them before you came back. I just felt so lonely on my own and the house is so big . . . I, well, here you are, love.' She held out a cup of tea, her way of smoothing things over, but Ruth refused to take it.

'Nice and milky, just the way you like it.' The spoon began to rattle in the saucer and tea slopped over the side of the cup. Ruth was out of her depth. She took the tea, not knowing what to say, and felt her anger curdle into guilt.

'There, that's better. I'll pack them away now you're back. Of course, I'll pack it all away . . .'

That night Ruth waited for a long time before she followed her mother up to bed. The shaving things were still on the shelf. She left the bathroom and took a step towards her mother's room, but the bar of light under the door went out. Ruth turned, walked with great care down the exact centre of the landing to her room and softly closed the door.

Chapter Six

'Welcome back, child.'

Awake into dank, heavy darkness. They are clustered ahead, mushroom-white skins gleaming in faint beams of dancing light.

'The beast is stronger now.'

'Soon it will come to our call.'

'Watch.'

They turn to face a shadowed entrance, leaning forward and trembling in concentration. She looks around for the source of the lights and sees other people lounging, as casual as a bus queue on a summer's day. Turning towards the creatures again, rage fills her, hot and clean, and a rush of blood charges her forward. Her fists fly. There is a wet thump and a rush of foul air. Her foot swings gracefully to crack into a leg and her knee slams into a pulpy white belly. She stops, breathless. One writhes on the floor; another hisses viciously, bent in pain. Grinning fiercely, she gathers her muscles for another charge.

Then all the strength drains out of her as the creatures turn. All they do is look at her with their slitted, lizard eyes, but it is enough. Every fear and nightmare she has lived through is there and to move would be to swim through jagged ice. When they finally discard her and look back at the entrance, she slumps to her knees.

The ground vibrates as the beast comes awake and starts to move. The pounding grows so loud and heavy, it seems to stamp its way into her brain. Sweat chills on her palms.

'No, please. I don't want to see it. Don't make me see it . . .'

Ruth woke with the pounding still in her head. 'We've lost, I'm lost,' she whispered to the pillow. Switching on the bedside lamp, she reached for her pencil and pad, but could only stare at the blank paper with eyes as dull as oil-filmed water. She gazed at the bottle of sleeping pills for a moment before reaching out and taking one. Even in a drugged sleep she could feel that power beating against the walls of her consciousness.

The next morning Ben was waiting at the gates of the garage. He put his arm round her shoulders and guided her into the tiny office.

'Bad, was it?'

Ruth told her dream. When she had finished, Ben picked up a squat brown teapot and poured two steaming mugs of tea. Ruth found a sugar-clogged spoon, stirred up a rippling whirlpool and stared into it until Ben broke the silence.

'At least you had a go at them,' he said.

'We might as well give up, Ben.' Her voice was small and dry, like a flurry of dead leaves. 'That thing they're calling on is too strong now. Even if we found the place, we couldn't do anything.'

'Don't be stupid. We've got to keep trying or be forever wondering whether we could've stopped it.' He kneaded his fist against his forehead. 'If we find the place, we can warn people and at least we'll know where you mustn't go.'

'But we don't know anything! What's going to happen? When is it going to happen? We don't know!'

Ben's hand shook as he reached for his tea. 'Don't.'

Ruth grabbed his hand in both of hers. 'Sorry, I'm sorry. It's just – I feel so desperate. There's something else. I don't know who to talk to about it . . .'

'Go on.'

'It's my mum. Since Dad died she's been strange. No, that's not true. She was all right at first – as all right as she could be in the circumstances – but since we moved here it's as if she's going further and further away from me. She doesn't care what I do any more; doesn't notice where I go or what time I get back. I thought she was just exhausted with the move and learning how to run the shop, but when I got back from Bodmin I found –' Ruth stopped and swallowed hard several times. Ben waited.

'She'd put his shaving things out in the bathroom and his dressing gown was hanging behind the door.

'You see, we only moved here because it was what Dad always wanted. Everyone told her it was a bad idea but she wouldn't listen. Now she's stuck down here with no friends, pretending he's still alive.' Ruth stopped because her voice had become so high and quavery, it was hurting her throat. She gripped Ben's hand hard enough to feel the bones grate together but the tears still came.

'Ruth, don't cry,' pleaded Ben. 'Come here.' He

pulled her to her feet and they hugged fiercely.

'Must go,' said Ruth eventually, her face still pressed into Ben's neck.

'OK.' Ben let his arms fall to his sides and Ruth turned to the door. On an impulse he called, 'Come for a meal tonight – I'll make a stew.'

It was the best thing he could have said. Ruth smiled for the first time that day and the thought of an evening with Ben sustained her all the way to the school gates.

She sidled into the schoolyard behind a group of third-years but Debbie spotted her and strolled over, flanked by Spaghetti-hair and Ian Ryder. She was impeccably made up and her hair was a length of black silk. They stopped in front of Ruth and Ian draped an arm loosely about Debbie's shoulders. She really is pretty, thought Ruth, distantly. They look good together.

'It's the townie who thinks she's too good for us.' Debbie smiled lazily, aware of the growing crowd. 'I hear she's been away for the week. Guess who else has been away for the week? Ben Treseder.'

'I'll bet he's had his engine well tuned. Did you show him your spark plugs? Want to have a look at my dipstick?' Ian's suggestive tones brought hoots of laughter. Ruth stared at him blankly, controlling her temper. They're only words, she told herself, only words.

Alice Beddows was watching the whole scene from the staffroom. Her fingernails tapped a rhythm of growing irritation on the sill. 'That Debbie creature,' she muttered, swinging away from the window. She spotted Geoffrey Edwards and opened her mouth to call him over, then shut it and turned to the telephone

93

instead. She dialled and waited. The receiver burbled quietly to itself, then clicked sharply.

'Headmistress? Alice Beddows here. It's about one of our fourth-year girls . . .'

At afternoon registration, trying to be discreet, Mr Edwards used his quiet voice as he bent towards Ruth. The room was silent within seconds. 'Mrs Sheraton wants to see you right away,' he whispered. Ruth could feel the wary glances of the form and made herself smile as she stood up. At the door she turned, looked directly at Debbie, pointed her hand like a gun and pretended to shoot.

'Come in,' rasped a voice when Ruth knocked. She opened the office door and peered through the smoke. Mrs Sheraton was leaning back in her chair with a cigarette trapped between her fingers. Even sitting down, she seemed to dance with nervous energy, flicking her cigarette every few seconds above an overflowing ashtray before any ash had had time to form.

'Take a seat,' said the headmistress, fixing her with a stare. Ruth sat, feeling like a rabbit caught in headlights. The chair was so low, her chin was level with the desk top and the headmistress was still staring, willing Ruth to look at her. She concentrated instead on Mrs Sheraton's wiry grey hair, which was whirled into a springy mass like a pan scourer, and thought of Ben.

'I don't think she likes you,' Ruth said that evening.

'The feeling's mutual,' said Ben. 'I hate the way she tries to dominate people. She thinks a problem crushed is a problem solved. Somebody should tell her ground glass can be deadly.' He scowled, remembering past battles.

'Ben, did you really tell her you couldn't wait to leave her school?'

'Well, she was prying.'

They were silent; Ben with his memories, Ruth in admiration that anyone could say such a thing to Mrs Sheraton. She scraped her plate clean and sat back, pushing her chair away from the table. 'That was delicious; and I love your flat. It's so . . .'

She looked about her, searching for the right word. The door at the top of the outside staircase opened straight on to a room that ran the length of the garage roof. The floorboards, walls and sloping ceiling were all painted white, increasing the sensation of space, and the curtains at the three windows were bright red. The whole place was scrupulously clean and very bare. Apart from the table and two chairs, there was a bookcase with a cassette radio and a collection of tapes on the top, a sagging armchair, a Calor gas fire and a single bed with a cover of the same bright red as the curtains. A hardboard partition hid a sink and a cupboard with a gas ring on top, and there was a curtained alcove next to the bed.

'. . . different,' finished Ruth lamely. 'It must be great to have a place of your own – you can do just what you want.'

'Cold on winter nights, though.'

'Do I have to go downstairs for the toilet?' asked Ruth, dreading a journey to the empty garage below, but Ben pointed to what looked like a walk-in cupboard. Inside was a tiny bathroom with just enough room for a toilet and an ancient shower unit.

When Ruth came out, the table had been cleared

and Ben was running water and rattling plates behind the screen. She began a leisurely circuit of the room. Behind the alcove curtain the shelves were neatly stacked with jeans, jumpers and shirts. Underneath were shoes, hiking boots, a rucksack and a rolled-up tent. Piled up against the opposite wall were the cleaning things for the flat. Nothing else. Where were the old annuals, the football trophies, the battered teddy? Ruth frowned, suddenly understanding why the flat seemed so bare. He had left his childhood at the farm.

'Coffee?' called Ben and Ruth hastily let the curtain drop.

'Yes, please.'

Not even a photograph? There was something framed above the bookcase and Ruth walked over. It was just a poster: a collection of vivid quilted and embroidered pictures. Nearly every one had words stitched along the top or bottom edge. She leaned closer to a collage of a village church surrounded by fields full of sheep and read, 'Canterbury CND wants life on earth'.

'Oh, I see. They're banners.'

'Great, aren't they?' asked Ben, handing over a mug of coffee.

'Thanks. Are you a member, then?'

'Yes, have been for years. It was Rosemary who got me started. What about you?'

'Well, no. But I agree with you.'

'So should anyone who hasn't got a death wish. Look out there,' he said, moving to the window. 'That's what we should be working on – wind and wave power.'

'I thought that was meant to be too expensive,' said

Ruth, dredging up a vague memory of a social studies lesson.

'Says who? And nuclear power isn't exactly bargain basement, you know. Anyway, it's not just the money. Can you imagine anything as stupid as building a nuclear power station without knowing how to get rid of the waste safely?'

'No . . . um . . .' Ruth groped for something to say. 'Do you go on any of those demonstrations? They must be fun. I've seen them on the TV. All those bands and balloons and jugglers.'

'Fun? The last one I went to was at an air base. We spent hours on a double decker – we couldn't afford a flash coach. The drop-off was in the middle of nowhere and we had to walk miles just to get there. Then we spent the afternoon wading through ankle-deep mud and avoiding the barbed wire, trying to surround the base. We did it, though,' he added, with quiet satisfaction.

'Why? I mean, do you think it changes anything?'

'I don't know. But you've got to fight for the important things, haven't you?'

'Yes,' said Ruth and concentrated on drinking her coffee. She had never cared enough about anything to give up her time and her comfort.

'What did Sheraton want, anyway?' asked Ben.

'Mrs Beddows brought it to her attention that I'm not integrating.'

'Not integrating.'

'That's right, not integrating.'

'Stupid woman.'

'One good thing, though; it's scared off Debbie's lot. I don't know how long that'll last but it's one less thing to cope with.'

'You're doing fine,' said Ben. He walked around the room, drawing the curtains against the early dark, then turned up the Calor gas fire. 'Come on,' he said, taking her hand. 'You can sit in the only armchair and I'll tell you about some of the places I want us to visit this Saturday. It's going to be a long day.'

'And a long week before that,' added Ruth.

They were both right. The week stuttered by with every night broken by the dream and Saturday was a confusing mess of stone circles, bus journeys, ancient forts and holy wells.

'Well, that was useless,' sighed Ben, watching the sun go down. His shoulders slumped. Ruth, sitting on a boulder and rubbing her aching feet, could hardly find the energy to answer. She stared across to the black silhouette of the Boswens longstone. Another dead end. 'What do we do now?' she asked.

Ben jumped to his feet and began to pace back and forth like a clockwork toy. 'These Saturday trips'll have to stop. We're just wandering around, counting on luck to take us to the right place. If only we had more to go on.'

With a big effort, Ruth marshalled her thoughts. 'What about a week trying to get more information? You step up the research and I'll really work on trying to pick up more clues from the dream. What do you think? Ben?' She held out her hands and he stopped his pacing to help her up. They stood close together against the wind and Ruth noticed the thin, sour smell of his breath, the red veins in his eyes. She smoothed the hair back from his forehead. 'What do you think?' she repeated.

'I think I'd like to be back on Bodmin Moor with

you,' he whispered and bent to rest his head on her shoulder.

That week, November made its presence felt with half-frozen rain and a high, keening wind that spent the afternoons tuning up for the nights. Ruth lay awake listening to its mournful songs at her window and Ben brushed it away in irritation as it sidled in under his door and flirted with the pages of his book. Each night it whipped up into a gale that shook the rooftops of the village and bounced huge waves against the cliffs. But the cliffs held firm – almost.

There was one finger of land that poked out into the sea where the currents were strong. The base of the cliff had been gradually eaten away, leaving a great weight of rock hanging above the waves. On the third stormy night the lighthouse beam found a tiny crack beginning to edge its way between the cliff and the overhang, following the fault lines of the granite. Each night after that, when the lighthouse beam swept across the cliffs, it lit up a crack that was a little longer and an overhang that leaned a tiny bit closer to the waves below.

The village struggled on, using the clear blue mornings to replace tiles on its battered roofs and hunt down stray dustbin lids. The storms were a talking point in the pub and the shops. Another talking point was Ben.

'No one's ever been so rude to me before,' hissed the librarian through the grille as she collected her TV licence stamp in the post office. The counter clerk tut-tutted. The queue leaned closer, silenced.

' "Young man," I said, "for the last time, I cannot let you take this many books out at once. Besides, one of these is a reference book." Well, you should have seen the look he gave me, Marjory. There was madness in that boy's eyes.'

Marjory gasped, the change forgotten in her damp palm, and frowned at someone thoughtlessly shuffling through a pile of leaflets.

The librarian tucked her chin into her neck and regarded Marjory knowingly before leaning forward to continue the saga. 'Nine books he had and do you know what they were all about?'

Marjory and the queue shook their heads.

'Ghosts, legends and unexplained disasters,' hissed the librarian, drawing in her chin again to watch the effect. 'Anyway, he turned round without another word, went across to the table and stayed there for the rest of the afternoon making funny notes on the back of a lot of my reservation cards.'

'What on earth does he want with those sort of books?' breathed Marjory.

'I dread to think,' replied the librarian, although she had thought of little else.

'I saw him walking down the street talking to himself,' chipped in someone from the queue. 'Like he was telling himself off. Kept smacking his fist against his forehead.'

'And that girlfriend of his looks like death warmed up. Have you seen her? My Paul says she fell asleep in maths the other day.'

'Something's going on,' said Marjory, and the queue nodded.

Something's going on, thought Mrs Davis the following Saturday when Ben and his rucksack did not appear at the back door, but then she was swept into the work of the shop and thought no more about it.

The morning was clear and bright, with the wind just starting to wake up after a hard night and no sign of the rain that had puddled the afternoons. Ruth, left alone with images of Friday night's dream, grabbed Rusty's lead and rushed him out of the house.

'He's out,' called the garage owner when she opened the office door. 'Gone to the library again. I think he's planning to move in there soon. Every lunch-hour he –' But Ruth had gone.

She took the walk she had grown to like, up to the lighthouse, then along the cliff edge towards the ruined engine houses. Rusty raced ahead then tore back, dancing and barking up into her face before rushing on again. When she reached the engine house where she had first met Ben, Ruth sat down and Rusty collapsed beside her, panting loudly and sniffing into the wind.

After a while she reached out and caressed his coat, rubbing his back and scratching behind his ears. Rusty licked her hand and laid his head across her thigh, sighing contentedly. They stayed there for a suspended time, warm and relaxed. The strengthening wind tugged at Ruth's hair and put neat partings in Rusty's coat before ruffling them away and starting again.

Suddenly Rusty stiffened, rolled over and leapt to his feet. He sniffed the air, staring intently out to sea, then strained his eyes along the cliffside path, the way they had come.

'What've you spotted?' asked Ruth, glancing lazily along the footpath but seeing nothing. Rusty whined at her, ran in a tight little circle and turned again to stare out to sea. He began to quiver and backed away from the cliff edge, rumbling uneasily in his throat.

Ruth sat up. A faint scuffling came from the spot where Rusty had been standing. Suddenly she was cold in the warm sunshine and the coppery taste of fear was in her mouth. She clambered to her feet and stood, fists clenched, ready to run. Nothing happened. Wiping her wet palms on her jeans, she took one step, then another, until she was at the edge. Still nothing moved.

Ruth let out her breath. 'Idiot,' she muttered and kicked at a tussock of grass. A furry brown ball exploded from under her feet and shot off down the cliff path. Rusty was dumbfounded. The rabbit was out of sight before he thought of lifting a paw.

Ruth collapsed in giggles, sinking to her knees on the path and looking straight into a pair of pale, watery eyes, just over the cliff edge. The slitted, lizard pupils reflected no light, showing instead absolute darkness within. The mouth split into a grin. Pointed teeth glinted.

Ruth screamed, then echoed her scream as she saw other pale figures clambering up towards her. To her left, some had already scrambled over on to the clifftop. She hurled herself backwards, rolled and jumped to her feet. The creatures paused to get their bearings, then formed into two packs. One group turned towards Rusty; the others, slowly confident, began to move in her direction.

Ruth backed off until she jarred to a halt with the rough stone of the engine house pressing into her shoulders. The creatures continued their slow advance. Keeping them in sight, Ruth slid down the wall until her fingers touched the ground. When both hands had found a heavy stone fragment, she eased back into a standing position. The creatures fanned out into a half-circle that trapped her against the wall, then stopped.

Rusty began to howl and Ruth risked a glance his way. He was surrounded by the creatures but he wasn't looking at them. His gaze was locked on her face. He was shaking.

Ruth flicked her eyes back and, just for an instant, the creatures in front of her rippled like reflections on water. She blinked and they were solid again. Ruth grew very still. Her mind was racing.

It was when I looked away and back . . . They were almost – not there. I wonder . . . ?

She turned her head slightly. There! The creatures right at the edge of her vision quivered and faded, their colours turning milky.

It's almost as though I'm projecting them. They're . . .

'. . . not really here! You're not really here!' she yelled.

A lisping snigger slithered around the semi-circle and they moved closer. Ruth swallowed hard and took a step forward.

'If I've brought you, I can make you go.'

She raised her fist with the rock lying heavy in it and took a deep breath. 'Get out of here!' she screamed.

The creatures did not flinch but Rusty answered her scream with a terrified yelp. She turned and saw that he was backing away from her towards the cliff edge, still surrounded by his own nightmare ring.

Ruth turned cold, made witless with shock. Before she could react, the group came to a stop a few feet from the cliff edge. An instant before it happened, Ruth realised what their next move would be. It was not a thought, not even a flash of words; she saw a picture, a moving picture that leapt into her mind with such clarity she was running in the same second.

She was halfway to Rusty when she fell. All the breath was knocked out of her. The outer edge of the cliffside circle slowly began to open out. Desperate, she crawled on. 'Rusty!' she croaked. 'Stay there. Don't go that way!'

The gap grew wider as the circle hinged back on itself, leaving the puppy a clear blue escape route. His howls stopped. Ruth could just see the back of his head; the delicate, vulnerable curve of his skull as he stared at the gap. Even in his great fear, he instinctively checked for the hidden trap.

'Rusty!' She called his name again in such an agony of hurt and love that he turned away from the edge to look at her. Ruth staggered to her feet. He saw her coming towards him, a rock still clenched in her fist, and a lonely howl trembled in his throat. He turned, bunched his muscles and leapt towards the gap, his russet coat feathering out from his body. With a flowing, oiled movement, he soared over the cliff; the creatures dissolved and flowed away with him. Ruth was left alone, staring at an empty blue sky.

Snuggled in the curve of the cliff, Mr Edwards gave a frustrated sigh. The past three weekends had provided fascinating bird-watching for the time of year, but today . . . It was as though something was keeping them away. Turning his back on the sea, he began unpacking his lunch. He stopped for a moment, idly watching the girl who was running along the cliff path to the village. Her auburn hair flamed in the sunlight and her long legs flew out behind her. She made an attractive picture.

The new girl, he thought, and was about to turn away when she looked behind her. Even from that distance he could read the panic in her face.

'What the – ?' He jumped to his feet, scanning the cliff path for her pursuer, but there was no one. Puzzled, he turned again to watch her until, still running, she disappeared from view.

With a mental shrug, he returned to his sandwiches, but they tasted of their plastic wrapping and the soup scalded his mouth. His back was tense and he shivered, suddenly aware of the solitude. He walked back to the village, stiff and controlled, denying a childish urge to keep glancing over his shoulder.

Chapter Seven

The voices of children floated in at her window. She lay in the peaceful warmth of her bed and listened. They were playing a skipping game and their words arrowed through the cold air.

'Ap – ple – pie – lem – on – tart –
Tell me – the name of – your – sweet – heart –
a – b – c – d – e – f –'

The slap of the rope and the thud of feet hitting the ground stopped. There was a confused muttering, followed by a piping shriek. 'F for Fiona! It's Fiona!'

'What, smelly Fiona? Wouldn't go near her.'

'Come on, then. Prove it!'

The rope resumed its steady beat and, when it was joined by pounding feet, the chant began again. 'Yes – no – yes – no – yes!' High laughter leapt into the air.

Ruth smiled and opened her eyes. Morning light filtered through her curtains and, as she sat up to draw them back, the room spun in a pleasantly lazy curve. Her arm seemed to stretch into the far distance before she could grasp the curtains and open them.

After a slight struggle, she focused on a small boy in the back lane as he bent to untangle the rope from his ankles. His ears were bright red. The game began again and the next child eyed the turning rope as though it were a snake, moving with it hypnotically.

A mongrel padded past and Ruth gazed sleepily after it. Then her eyes widened as the sight tugged at something submerged in the depths of her memory. It came bobbing to the surface, bloated and horrible. Rusty was dead.

The floodgates opened and everything came rushing back. She saw herself stumbling into the shop, screaming in a tired, repetitive way. She saw her mother's face, mouth stretched in a horrified O, skin paled to a cheesy white. She saw Debbie's father, looking as sly as a water-rat and holding out a syringe. She saw the needle sink into her arm and watched them both float away, talking about hysteria and how it was quite common after a shock. They had grown as tiny as ants before the light went out.

There had been the strangest dreams. She swam through caves whose spongy walls were veined with bright colours. So warm. So mindless. Once in the night, she surfaced in her room and panicked, screaming for the peace again. Her mother was there with tablets and water and Ruth spiralled down into the caves again as the wind and the rain beat against her window.

Now, it was calm outside and bright. The world had moved on. Ruth lay back and pulled the covers over her head. She cried for a long time until finally her sobs became shuddering breaths and the tears stopped. She got out of bed and made her way downstairs.

'What happened, Ruthie? I mean exactly. Can you tell me?'

'But I did tell you . . . didn't I?'

'I know Rusty went over the cliff, that's all. It took me a while to get you to stop screaming. Then the doctor arrived and gave you an injection and, well,' Mrs Davis shrugged, 'here we are. I just need to know what else happened.'

Ruth looked at her mother, who was sitting at the kitchen table with her hair still in curlers. She looked out of the open back door at the washing blowing on the line and she listened to the church bells calling from the village. I was awake, she thought. I know I was.

'Nothing else happened, Mum. Rusty was chasing something through the grass – a mouse or a rabbit – it was too fast for me to see. He lost his footing at the edge.' Tears scratched at her throat and she stopped.

'So, no one tried to, um, hurt you? There wasn't – a man?'

'No. There wasn't a man.'

Mrs Davis visibly relaxed. 'Poor Rusty. At least it was quick – he probably didn't even realise what was happening.'

Ruth nodded, but she was still hearing his terrified howls as the creatures surrounded him.

'Ruthie, I have to tell you this before you get your hopes up. There's no chance of, you know, finding him.'

'I know that, Mum,' said Ruth, remembering how Rusty had launched himself off the cliff. There would have been no friendly ledges on the way down for him.

'Mr Penhale says there's a strong undertow all along that stretch of coast. Anything which falls in gets taken out to sea.'

108

'Mr Penhale? Mum, how does he know? You told him?'

'Well, no –'

'Who else knows?'

'Ruthie, there were people in the shop when you ran in. They saw you. They heard.'

Ruth leaned forward until her face was resting on the warm wood of the table top, then she wrapped her arms around her head.

'That Ben Treseder phoned last night,' said Mrs Davis, changing the subject. 'He was all for coming up to see you right away but I put him off. He's coming later this morning instead, after the doctor's been.'

'Oh no, not Pascoe again?'

'Doctor Pascoe, please. He's just calling to make sure you're back to normal.'

'Mum, you can see I am,' said Ruth, lifting her head to emphasise the point.

'Look, I didn't ask him to come. He told me he would – That'll be him now,' said Mrs Davis, jumping up at the sound of the doorbell. 'Oh, my curlers! Where's that scarf?'

Five minutes later, Dr Pascoe was back on the doorstep, lecturing her mother on the excitability of teenage girls. 'Especially if they're, shall we say, highly strung,' he finished, glancing at Ruth. She had a vision of herself hanging from a rope ten feet in the air, looked away to hide a smile and there was Ben. He was standing across the street, shuffling his feet and glaring at Dr Pascoe's back.

Ruth stopped smiling. She took a step back into the shadowy hallway, then another step. By the time her

109

mother closed the door after the doctor, Ruth had eased her way into the sitting room. When the doorbell rang, she did not move and when her mother called from the hallway, she did not answer. She listened as Mrs Davis clumped up the stairs, still calling.

'Ruthie?' The voice trailed downstairs again after the flapping slippers and, finally, the sitting-room door opened.

'There you are. Didn't you hear me? Ben's here.'

Ben stepped into the room, his dark face softening as he caught sight of her, but Ruth was rearranging a group of pottery kittens on the mantelpiece and did not turn around. The clock ticked loudly. Ben looked a question at Mrs Davis.

'Um, I'll make a pot of tea,' she said, and ducked out of the room.

'What happened?' asked Ben.

'Oh, I'm sure you've heard. Everyone else has.'

'No, I mean what really happened?'

'They climbed up over the cliff. They killed Rusty. Or I did.'

'You killed . . . ? How?'

'They'd surrounded us and . . . and I picked up a rock, to fight them with if they came any nearer. Then I saw he'd backed away right to the edge, so I ran towards him, with this rock in my fist, screaming at him to stop – and he jumped. He was terrified. But,' her voice rose to a wobbly high, 'I don't know whether he was terrified of them, or of me. I'm not sure whether he could see them.'

'But, they were there?'

'I don't know! I could see them. They seemed as solid as this.' She thumped the mantelpiece. 'But,

110

just before he jumped, I thought it was me, making them happen. I thought that maybe when I looked away, they – stopped . . . So I tried shouting them away, but all it did was scare Rusty into jumping. He went over the edge and they just . . . disappeared.'

Ben came and put his arms around her but she stood, inert, like a stuffed toy. 'What is it?' he asked, taking a step back.

Ruth turned back to the pottery kittens.

'Oh, come on. I thought we'd got past this sort of game. If you're mad at me, just tell me. Ruth . . . ?' He tailed off, feeling his bafflement starting to fray into anger.

Still Ruth was silent. Ben stood in the middle of the quiet room holding down the shout that wanted to leap out of his mouth. After two long minutes he said, 'Call in at the flat when you're feeling better, OK?' He turned and marched towards the door.

'Where were you, Ben?'

'What? I was at the library . . . Look, I didn't realise. I didn't pick up anything, not like when you're dreaming. You know I would've come if I'd had any idea.'

'That's just it; you had no idea. I'm the one who has the dreams. I'm the one whose dog got killed. And I want it to end. I don't want any more research or visits or anything. What happened to Rusty – maybe it was a warning. I just think we should back off for a while.'

'You mean back out,' said Ben softly.

'Look, you can call me a coward, but that's what I want. I want you to stop.'

'Ruth, I'm sorry for Rusty, but –'

'He wasn't your dog, though, was he?'

'You're blaming me, aren't you? Aren't you?'

111

'All right, yes! Yes! I'm blaming you.'

'You make me sick,' said Ben and he left the room, closing the door very quietly behind him.

Monday's sky was the colour of grime on a shirt collar. Ruth could feel it sulking just above her head as she trudged to school. She had nearly given in when her mother suggested a day off to recover, but her need for something to do was greater than her need for rest. Besides, her absence would only fuel the gossip. She pretended not to notice a tiny hope that was jumping up and down at the back of her mind, squeaking, perhaps they haven't heard.

Crossing the main street, Ruth saw Alison's tall figure detach itself from the group ahead to wait for her. It was something to focus on as she walked stiffly past the garage gates.

'Hi.' Alison's glance was slightly wary. 'Are you all right?'

'Why shouldn't I be?' asked Ruth, but her heart fell. They knew.

'Look, I stopped to tell you what Debbie's been saying. Just so you know. She says her dad had to go out to your house on Saturday because you were hysterical and your mum didn't know how to stop you. She heard her dad telling her mum about it when he got back. I'll bet her ears were tuned in like radars all weekend – unless she's making it up?'

Ruth shook her head.

'Oh. Well, Debbie's telling some really colourful stories about the state you were in.'

'Is that all? You mean she hasn't found out about my head transplant or . . . or the escaped convict hiding in our attic?'

Alison didn't laugh. 'I'm sorry about Rusty. He was a lovely dog. Come to the lab at lunchtime if you like, for a break. It's going to be a tough day.'

That evening Ruth walked into the kitchen and sat at the table still in her school coat. She watched shadows grow in the corner where Rusty's basket and bowl had stood, and she listened to faint voices and the bleep of the till from the shop. She tried to scrub the day from her mind but it was still squatting there, slimy and toadlike, when Mrs Davis found her sitting in the chilly dark.

They had tea in the sitting room with only the blare of the television to fill the quiet spaces. Ruth let the quiz shows stuff her head with tinsel; glitter stopped her from seeing the toad. She sank down into a chair and prepared to let the television eat away the hours before bed.

'Wake up, Ruthie. I'm going up now. Are you coming?'

Ruth opened her eyes and saw her mother standing by the chair in dressing-gown and curlers. 'Oh, is that the time?' She struggled to her feet, aware that she had hardly spoken all evening, but her mother was smiling.

'It's been nice tonight,' she said. 'You know, homely. Just what you needed.'

Ruth blinked. *How can she say that? It's been awful.* She looked at her mother as a stranger might and saw how the skin of her face was beginning to slacken, making the corners of her mouth droop. Her nose was mapped with tiny, broken veins and there were deep crescents of shadow under her eyes. A day in the shop had left her smelling of onions and soap powder.

The memory of a night years ago surprised Ruth like a forgotten photograph falling from the pages of a book. There had been a smell of roses and excitement in the air. Ruth had been in bed when her mother came in, wearing an emerald-green evening dress that rustled silkily when she moved. As she leaned forward for a goodnight kiss, jewels danced at her ears and throat and her shoulders gleamed in the light from the landing. Over the cool, milky curve of her neck, Ruth had seen her father framed in the doorway, dark and nervously tailored. A big night out.

The memory left behind such a longing that Ruth reached out and grabbed her mother, nuzzling into her neck as she had done then. Only now, Mrs Davis was the small one and Ruth had to stoop to reach. She held her mother tight, wanting to heal the loss and the waste and the distance between them, but the hug became awkward and soon Mrs Davis stepped back, smiling self-consciously.

'Right, I must go to bed before I drop. What about you?'

Ruth turned away. 'I'll finish watching this first,' she said. Sinking into the easy chair, she stared at the television until the final credits had faded from the screen.

Two o'clock in the morning. Rain pelted against the window as Ruth lay in the dregs of her nightmare, trying to catch her breath. The beast was getting closer every time.

She thought of Ben, awake in his long, white room, cursing her for her lack of fight. She thought of Rusty and how she had failed him. She thought of how easy it had been for Debbie to bully her and suddenly her self-disgust was too much to bear. She jumped out of bed and stood there while three blasts of wind, one after the other, shook the window in its frame.

The house had that middle-of-the-night feel to it. The rules had changed and humans had no business to be up and about. It was the turn of spiders, mice and all the other tenants. Ruth remembered the white creatures and turned to scuttle back under the covers. But as her hand touched the quilt, she thought, this is all their fault, and stopped dead, shot through with a long flame of anger. It was as though a match had been put to a blowtorch heavy with fuel. All the fear and shame that had collected inside her began to burn so fiercely, the small room could not contain the blaze.

Ruth flung open the door, marched down the stairs and into the kitchen, coming to a halt at a row of coat-hooks. She grabbed the old sweater her mother wore for latenight shelf-stocking and fought her way into it. Then she pulled her bicycle cape over her head, stuck her bare feet into a pair of wellingtons and stumbled to the back door, tucking in her pyjama legs as she went. The bolts slid back easily, the door flew open and she ran outside.

A gust of wind caught the back door and slammed it twice before the latch dropped and it stayed shut. Mrs Davis turned over and muttered in her sleep, throwing out an arm to the other side of the bed. Her hand fumbled across the empty pillow for a moment before she sighed and settled down again. The noise of the storm was just a backdrop to her dreams.

Out in the open, Ruth's hair was plastered to her head in seconds and the wind cuffed at her until she was dizzy. The din of the storm was so steady, it was almost like silence. She shielded her eyes against the stream of water running from her hair and looked for a way through the dark confusion. A faint glimmer gave away the next street-light on the road down to the village and she made her way towards it, not stopping until she reached the lamppost. She leaned there for a moment, squinting through the rain to find the next light, then, wiping the water from her eyes, she took a deep breath and set off again.

The lampposts took her all the way down to the crossroads and up the cliff road towards the school. She stepped out of her wellingtons three times and both feet were scratched and muddy, but she did not stop until she reached the lamppost outside the school. It was the last one. The only light on the road ahead came from the lighthouse beam, which slipped past on its weak, wavery search every fifteen seconds.

Ruth hesitated for the first time. In Coventry the streets had never been truly dark; not like the pitchy blackness that waited beyond the lamppost. Then she thought of Rusty and anger returned, burning so fiercely that her doubts frizzled up. She stepped out of the circle of light and headed for the cliffs.

The journey was difficult but, like a lot of things, not as hard as the imagining. Her feet told her the difference between tarmac and grass and the lighthouse beam gave her a direction. Ruth's biggest battle was against the wind. The gale came shrieking over the cliffs, blasting icy rain into her face. It would slacken suddenly, then send a gust from one side like a huge left hook, so that she was forever stumbling off balance.

By the time Ruth had reached the lighthouse, she

was exhausted and shivering. Sheltering in the lee of the boundary wall, she tried to catch her breath and rub the cold out of her face. Every time the lighthouse beam swept past, she peered along the cliff path, working out the easiest way through the rocks and grass to the edge. At last she stood up and felt her way along the wall until the wall ran out.

It was like a game of giant's footsteps. The powerful lamp made its slow circle through the night and, for as long as it stayed to light her way, Ruth scrambled through the sodden grass and rain-slick boulders. When the light went, she crouched in the howling dark and waited for it to come back. Eight circles later, she was standing with her legs braced against the wind and the cliff edge a few steps away. She knew exactly what she was going to do. She was going to declare war.

She bent and levered a chunk of granite out of the earth, ignoring the insects that scuttled over her hands. It felt good to hold; rough and heavy. She hefted it, feeling the dangerous weight of it, letting the anger burn through her.

It was like throwing a cardboard replica; so easy. The rock cleared the cliff edge and flew out over the sea. She took a step forward, imagining the rock smashing into the creatures below. Her anger turned white hot. I can do anything, she thought. Another step forward and she began to shout.

'Right, you slimy little murderers! I know you're out there somewhere. That was just for starters, do you hear? I've had enough. You've got a fight on your hands now, you wormy monsters!' She bent for another rock and hurled it with all her strength.

'I'm going to get you. You wait, you –'

117

She broke off, sucked in breath to scream and choked on rainwater. Her arms had been gripped from behind and with one fierce tug, her feet went out from under her. Her head banged against something cold and wet and rubbery as she was dragged backwards away from the cliff.

Dumped on the ground, she clambered to her feet and turned, ready to take them on. But there were no creatures silhouetted against the approaching lighthouse beam. Standing in front of her was the dark bulk of a man in a sou'wester. His arms came up, reaching for her.

Ruth stumbled backwards in her ill-fitting wellingtons, suddenly afraid; then the lighthouse beam reached them and she recognised Ben. His mouth was moving but she could hear nothing because the wind was flicking his words away like crumbs. She stared. Ben shook his head, took her hand and began to steer their stormy way home.

In her bedroom, Ruth sat as though drugged while Ben stripped off her muddy pyjamas, towelled her dry and wrapped her in the quilt from the bed. He worked fast and silently, aware of Mrs Davis snoring gently just down the landing. When it was done, he sat next to her on the bed, shivering inside the clammy weight of his own wet clothes. He started to whisper, trying to force his words through the exhaustion that was smothering her like treacle.

'Ruth – Ruth, listen. I'm sorry. You mustn't do that again. I'm sorry. I didn't see how upset you were. Are you listening? Promise me you won't try that again?'

'What?' Ruth opened her eyes and stared. 'You

don't think I was going to jump? No, no, I was angry. I wanted to kill them.'

'Oh.' Ben looked embarrassed.

'And Ben, I'm the one who's sorry. I've been pathetic. But I feel different now: determined. OK?'

'OK, we'll start again. Only this time, let's go through the books and everything together, right? I've been acting like I'm the great expert, but they're your dreams. Mind you,' he grinned, 'I have been working on an idea . . .'

'Oh, come on, tell me. Then I can get some sleep.'

'It is only an idea, though. It's mostly guesswork and I've got no real proof, only clues –'

'Ben! Just tell me. I can see you're bursting to.'

'OK. The place has got to be next to the sea and it's got to be local.'

'Go on.'

'The creatures came out of the sea to get Rusty, didn't they? And the way you described them – all pale and stinking of dead fish – it reminded me of something that lives deep in the sea.'

'But I only said they smelled horrible, like a dead jellyfish I found once. I didn't say – I mean, you're making a bit of a jump from that to sea creatures. Besides, I'm not sure whether they actually climbed out of the sea –'

'So why did you go there tonight?'

'It . . . it just seemed – right.'

'Exactly!'

'Shhh. My mum . . .'

'Sorry. Now, think about the sites we've been to so far. All inland. Even if it's just been a little way inland, none of them've been right next to the sea. And the place must be local –'

119

'Because of Bodmin Moor, right? It was more than just no dreams there, wasn't it? As though we'd stepped out from under a cloud and – oh, Ben. I've just remembered something. That first dream I had after we came home, they said, "Welcome back, child". Do you see? As if I'd been out of their reach.'

'Yes! Yes, it all fits in. Now, what we need to do is take the distance from the village to Jack and Rosemary's place – we know their range doesn't extend beyond that – mark it on a map from the lighthouse up and down the coast, and just pick out all the likely spots along that line.'

He went on whispering his hopes at her but Ruth was as near sleep as she could be with her eyes open. Still cocooned in the quilt, she slumped sideways until her head rested on the pillow. There was one unanswered question buzzing around in her brain like a mosquito, but she was too tired to catch it. Her eyes closed.

Ben leaned over and kissed her, very softly, on the mouth. Then he was gone, creeping silently down to his boots by the kitchen door.

Chapter Eight

'Anyone seen Ruth Davis?' Mr Edwards looked up, his hand poised over the register. The class looked at him, at one another and back to him. Finally there were some muttered denials. As Mr Edwards bent to the register again, Debbie hissed in a stage whisper, 'Let's hope she's gone back to Coventry.'

'I believe you've already sent her there,' he snapped and could have bitten his tongue.

Debbie opened her eyes wide and batted her lashes. 'What do you mean, sir?'

'Come along now. It has been noticed how you, ah, how you teased her yesterday about that business at the weekend.'

'What, ah, business was that, sir? I don't, ah, know what you mean, sir.'

'Oh, never mind. Let's try to get through the register, shall we?' said Mr Edwards as decisively as he could. But Debbie was not about to let such easy prey escape. By the time their teacher left the room, he had the laughter of the whole class at his heels.

Ruth slid a look round the bus to check for watchers before she yanked off her school tie and stuffed it deep into her bag. Then she buttoned up her raincoat to hide the blazer beneath and turned to Ben.

He looked exhausted. The skin around his eyes was a raw pink, while his tan looked dull and muddy. He was so excited, he could barely keep still, but he was watching her with a new wariness; testing the air.

Ruth wanted to put her hands to his face and stroke the doubt away. She wanted to say, forget the bad track record – you can trust me now, I've changed; but she had learned about the distance between words and actions. Instead, she reached for his hand, lacing their fingers together. 'Well?' she said.

'Well?' echoed Ben. 'You feeling OK after your stroll through the storm?'

Ruth smiled. 'I ache. And I feel – empty.'

'But still determined?'

'Oh, yes. Still determined.'

'Good. Because I've come up with an idea –'

'Will it explain why I'm sitting here with you when five minutes ago I was on my way to school?'

Ben flapped his free hand impatiently. 'I was working on it after I got back last night –'

'Now that's something else I want to ask you about.'

Ben sighed. 'Go on, then.'

'It was bothering me last night, but I was too tired to think straight. What on earth were you doing out on the cliffs?'

'No mystery,' said Ben. 'Call it coincidence. I was awake, as usual, after your nightmare and standing at the window, wondering that the hell I was going to do about it all. There were no lights on in the flat, so I could see into the road. Suddenly there you were, hanging on to that lamppost opposite the garage gates. I banged on the window but you were off, stomping up the road in those stupid wellies.'

'So you followed me?'

'Oh, but you were fast. Don't know how you did it in that storm. I only took a minute to get dressed but you were gone. I knew it must be the cliffs; that road doesn't go anywhere else. So I just kept going. Then I saw you in the lighthouse beam, right at the edge, and,' he shrugged and put on a bad American accent, 'the rest is history.'

'Thanks for coming after me. You didn't have to. I mean, when you came round on Sunday, I virtually told you to get lost.'

'That's history too,' said Ben. 'Now can I tell you what I've come up with? I got the maps out last night –'

'Did you get any sleep?'

'Didn't want any. I found one place, just below Padstow, and it meets all the conditions. Within the distance, right on the beach, and it's an iron-age burial site.' Ben craned past her to peer through the grimy bus window. 'Not far now. Just a few more miles.'

'But, Ben, wait a minute. What about the cliffs where Rusty died? That's the only place I've ever seen them, except in my dreams. Shouldn't we start there?'

'I thought of that, but there's nothing marked on the maps all along that stretch, not even a standing stone. It's all mining. No, it must be somewhere else.'

'You mean they travelled to the cliffs from somewhere else? How?'

'Travelled? What do you think they did? Swam?

Caught the bus? Look, you've got to stop thinking of them in such a solid way. If they can get inside your dreams, a trip up the coast isn't going to cause them much bother, is it? Come on, Ruth. You can't have it all in black and white. A thing like this, we have to go on guesswork.'

'I know, I know. Anyway, it's always closed in and dark and damp in the dreams – nothing like a clifftop.'

'And remember, you've walked along those cliffs a few times before and never picked up any bad feelings.'

'Yes, but that's true about all the places we've been so far. I'm not so sure about this metal-detector theory any more.'

'It could be that we haven't found the right place yet. It's all just –'

'Guesswork. I know.'

Ben smiled and squeezed her hand. 'Do me a favour? Wake me up when we've got through Newquay?' He lifted the rucksack on to his knees and, using it as a pillow, rested his head on his arms and closed his eyes.

The bus left them stranded in a flat wasteland of campsites and golf courses. An icy grey drizzle oozed its way out of the sky and seeped into their clothes as they trudged down the empty road to the dunes.

Ruth went into the neatly excavated site alone. Some of the bodies had been left where they were found, sealed by a window of glass. They were curled into a crouch, all pointing to the magnetic North, and their skulls had been broken for their souls to climb out. One young girl lay in her slate-slab coffin with two pet mice to keep her company.

They were just bundles of bone, seven thousand years old, but Ruth still felt as though she were spying into someone's bedroom. She pushed on, touring the whole place before she joined Ben on the beach. Under the drizzle, the sand had formed a dark, wet crust and the sea heaved, oily and sullen.

'Nothing,' said Ruth. 'Just sad and lonely.' She felt utterly deflated.

Ben was scowling at the sand and gouging a channel through it with the toe of his boot. 'I really thought . . . It seemed to be just the place.' He sighed and shoved his hands deep into his jacket pockets.

Resisting an impulse to curl up on the sand, Ruth turned to stand in front of him. She slipped her arms around his waist, pushing her hands under his jumper to warm them. 'Hey, come on. What is it you always say? One more place to cross off the list?'

She kissed him on the mouth and he pulled her close, pressing her face against his cold, stubbly cheek. 'Tell you what,' she said, 'got any coffee in that rucksack?'

'Of course. And a packet of biscuits.'

'What are we waiting for? Back to the bus shelter. And when we get home we'll get stuck into those books.'

'Slave-driver.'

'I told you,' said Ruth. 'I'm determined.'

'I still can't get over it, Ruthie. You've never done anything like this before. Honestly, I don't understand it.' Mrs Davis shook her head and went back to her VAT forms, but turned round again almost immediately. 'And fancy getting off the bus right in front of Mr Pugh, when you'd just missed his history lesson! I don't know how you thought you were going to get away with it in a place this size.'

Ruth said nothing. Her mother had been worrying at the subject for the last three hours and she had used up her stock of apologies. She gritted her teeth and sent the iron clicking and thumping its way round another shirt. Washing steamed on the clothes-horse and the kitchen was heavy with the smell of clean, pressed cotton.

'I'll never forget that phone call from the school. It was the headmistress, you know. The headmistress!' Mrs Davis squared up to the table again, rustling her paperwork in a businesslike manner.

Ruth glanced at the clock. Only five minutes to go. She grabbed her school skirt and tried to concentrate on ironing perfect pleats.

The doorbell broke the silence at exactly seven o'clock.

'I'll get it,' said Mrs Davis firmly. Ruth waited for a few seconds after the kitchen door had closed, then sprinted across the room and silently opened it a crack.

'Hello, Mrs Davis.'

'Ben.'

'In the kitchen, is she?'

'Just a minute. I'd like a quick word.'

Ruth clapped a hand across her mouth. *Here we go*.

'Now, don't think I'm not grateful, you know, that you keep her company when no one else will –'

Oh Mum!

'– and that holiday did her the world of good, but –

well, I didn't like what happened today. Not one bit.'

Ruth bit down on her knuckles and waited for the explosion.

'Sorry, Mrs Davis,' said Ben mildly.

'Oh. You are? I mean, I should hope you are. Well . . . um, I know you're working now and you might not think school is that important –'

Oh, God. If she knew how much he'd wanted to stay on.

'– but Ruth was having a hard job settling in as it was and now she's on report for a week.'

'I'm really sorry, Mrs Davis. It won't happen again.'

'No, it won't. Because I'm grounding her. No more days out. And it's no use objecting –'

'Whatever you say, Mrs Davis.'

'Really? Oh, well, in that case. You're welcome to come here, of course, especially since you're helping her with her history project. You do see, don't you, that I'm trying to do what's right for her?'

'I understand.'

'Well, let's stop wasting time here. You get those books through to the kitchen and I'll make a pot of tea.'

'That was brilliant!' said Ruth as soon as she and Ben were alone. 'You won her right over. She wasn't expecting that, you know. She's heard all the stories about your temper from the customers.'

'I meant what I said. Why should I get angry with her when she's only trying to look after you? I know it's not going too well between you, but at least she still cares.'

'Yeah, I suppose so,' Ruth agreed, remembering what Rosemary had said about Ben's mother. 'You know, she's enjoying this in a funny way; having a normal problem she can actually do something about. I mean, she couldn't do much against nightmares. Or death,' she added, glancing over at the coat-rack.

'Your dad's jacket?' asked Ben, following her gaze. 'What about the other stuff?'

'All still there. But she took Rusty's basket and bowl out to the shed straight away. Actually told me it was the best thing to do. Sometimes I think I should do the same with Dad's things but then I think, well, that's in a totally different league. You wouldn't treat a broken leg the same way as a bruised toe, would you? Oh, I don't really know what to do.'

Ben reached across the table and took her hand. 'Perhaps if you just give her some more time? She might do it herself, one day.'

Ruth nodded and blew her nose.

'OK? Now, what about this research? I can hardly keep my eyes open after last night, but I'm willing if you are.'

November tipped over into December that week, and it turned bitterly cold. Frost flowers grew over village windows every night and gritting lorries rumbled along the roads. Out by the cliffs, the granite overhang was still poised above the sea, but a deepening crevice was surely splitting it away from the main rock face. The water which seeped into cracks and flaws each day turned to ice at night, expanding as it froze. It was as though a wedge was being slowly driven into a cracked log. The breach grew broader and more fault lines opened up.

The build-up to Christmas got underway, but Ruth and Ben hardly noticed. They worked together every spare minute, only leaving the kitchen to search the library shelves for new possibilities, scanning history and legend for clues. Then back through the early dark to spread out their hopes on the table again.

Mrs Davis left them alone. She spent her evenings in the dimly lit shop, sorting out Christmas stock. She stacked the shelves with rich, dark plum puddings, hung stockings full of chocolate from the counter and arranged Christmas-tree baubles in nests of tissue paper, like clutches of fragile eggs. Her movements were calm and methodical but her throat muscles ached from swallowing down memories of the Christmas before.

She began to cry in her sleep. Not gentle little sobs, but great, ugly wails that grew louder and louder until she snapped awake with tears and mucus smeared across her face. She took to sitting by the kitchen stove into the early hours, rather than let sleep take away her self-control. She would make pots of tea and open packets of biscuits and tell herself that things were looking up. They were. All right, it was hard work and business wasn't as good as she'd hoped, but at least Ruth was better now, even though she was missing Rusty. Going to school every day, working hard every evening. No mention of nightmares for weeks . . . Yes, Ruth would be fine, she would be fine; just like Brian had always wanted.

'Sorry I'm late,' said Ben, swinging the back door shut with his foot and dumping a pile of library books on the kitchen table. 'I hate Friday afternoons. They all suddenly remember they're going away for the weekend and wander into the garage asking for last-minute tyre changes and oil checks. Give us a cuddle. I'm freezing.'

Ruth walked towards him, then stopped, wrinkling her nose. 'Phew! What's that smell?'

'Oh, hell,' said Ben, sniffing his hands. 'Antifreeze. I've been pouring the stuff into radiators all day.'

'Smells like cat pee. Go and wash it off.'

'Oh, come on, it's not that bad. Some aftershaves are worse than this. Give us a cuddle first.'

'Get lost!'

'I knew it; she loves me.' Ben grinned and turned to the kitchen sink. 'Got some more books,' he said, running hot water into the bowl. 'That was another hold-up. It's amazing how popular the library gets in cold weather. The reading room was crammed with pensioners trying to save on their heating bills. It was daggers-drawn over the *National Geographic*. And as for the chairs next to the radiators, well . . .'

He turned back to Ruth, hands dripping, and the smile was switched off his face.

One of the books lay open on the table and Ruth stood, ruler straight, staring down at it with her hands clamped over her mouth.

'Ruth!'

She turned to him and lowered her hands. Her fingers left imprints that flushed red against her white face. 'We've found it, Ben,' she whispered. 'It's one of the creatures.'

Ben grabbed the book. It was only a rough sketch but there were the lizard eyes, the gaping mouth. He stared, and felt an icy chill sigh across the back of his neck.

'Read what it says, Ben.'

'Um . . . "Sketched by an eighteenth-century tin miner who claimed to have seen this creature after a seam collapsed, killing thirty-four men and boys."' He broke off and stared at Ruth. 'A tin mine. It's going to be a tin mine.'

'Yes. In the dreams, that's where I am, isn't it? That's why they're so clammy and pale: they live underground – Oh!'

Ruth jumped up and scurried to the back door. With shaking hands she turned the heavy old key and scraped home the bolts. Then she ran to the sink and leaned across it to pull the curtains over a black square of window.

'What are you doing?'

'Ben, they could be out there now –'

'No, I don't think so. It says here they're always seen in or around mines. They're not going to come walking into your kitchen. This isn't part of their reality –'

'Of course they're real! The miner saw them too.'

'I didn't say they weren't real. I said they're not part of this reality. They're – fear shapes. Fear made solid. Look, come and sit down with me.' Ben picked up the book. 'It says here that miner was the sole survivor. Just think what he went through. He was all alone, in the dark, underground. The mates he'd been working with were all dead. He must've been terrified. It doesn't say how long he was down there or whether he had food and water. He could've been hurt or trapped . . .

'Do you see? His mind must've been on a different level, like yours is when you're dreaming –'

'Oh, great. So you're saying they're all in the mind now?'

131

'No! That's how that idiot doctor would dismiss it. I'm saying perhaps your mind has to be on a different level to reach their reality, like . . . going in a lift to another floor. Here's something else. Listen, "There have been persistent rumours about creatures like this ever since the start of deep-rock mining in Cornwall." There, you see? He was primed.'

'What, you mean he was expecting to see them?'

'Yes. He must've heard all the stories –'

'But I haven't. I haven't heard all the stories and I still dreamed about them. But I suppose that's where your telepathy theory fits in; picking up echoes.'

'Yes, and added to that, they're what everyone expects to find in a dark place. You know, all white and slimy. Uncle Jack's always talking about parallels. He says stories and myths are the same everywhere because they're about the basics – love, hate, revenge, fear . . . People have always been scared of dark places and what might be hidden there, so they trap the fear in a story. You see, even if you haven't heard the Cornish stories, you've heard fairy tales. You've heard stories about bogeymen and goblins. What about Gollum in *The Hobbit*? And another thing –'

Ruth thumped the table. 'Ben! Stop complicating it all with theories. You're making my head hurt. One thing I am sure about, my dreams are a warning. That's real enough and that's what we've got to solve. Let's have a look at that book again. There must be more . . . Here. "Miners blamed these creatures for earth falls or floodings, claiming they had the power to make the rock move."'

Ruth stopped reading. She marked the spot with her finger and looked up at Ben without really seeing him. 'Wait a minute . . . In my dreams, they keep talking about disturbing the beast. They must mean the mine, mustn't they? That's why I can feel the ground shaking. And that noise, that grinding – it must be rock against rock!'

Ruth began to read again. ' "The creatures are rumoured to change shape or vanish if approached –" That's just what they did when I saw them that day with Rusty and –' She broke off and stared at Ben with huge eyes.

'What? What's wrong?'

Ruth swallowed. 'I saw them at the cliffs. It wasn't underground, it wasn't dark. It was a sunny day.'

'OK,' said Ben slowly, 'so it was light – but that doesn't mean . . . You were on your own, weren't you? And you were already very frightened. You were thinking about them before you saw them – you told me that. Anyway, the book says in or around mines, and that part of the cliffs is around mines. Wait a minute!' Ben slapped his forehead with the palm of his hand. 'I really can't believe how thick I've been.'

'Ben, you haven't been –'

'Oh yes? Wait till you hear this. I've just remembered something, something I knew all the time, but I didn't have enough brainpower to make the connection. The cliff where Rusty died – I've been round that bit of coast a few times, by boat. If you look at those cliffs from the sea, there are little openings in them. They look like caves but they're not natural. They're very old mine tunnels – centuries old. People call them the Old Men's Workings. No wonder you saw them there. Plenty of fear and death and disaster seeping out of those tunnels – hundreds of years of echoes.'

'Do you think –?'

'Ah, don't start asking me what I think. I think I'd better leave the thinking to you from now on; I'm a dead loss at it. Anything else in there?'

Ruth began to read again. ' "To this day, miners will not whistle in a mine, believing that the creatures hate the cheerful sound. If they are working a dangerous seam, they will leave food in an attempt to pacify the creatures." That's it.'

'Are you sure? Look in the index. No, look at the contents page.'

'Ben! Don't sit there telling me what to do. What about the other books?'

'Sorry,' said Ben, pulling the pile towards him and splitting it in half. 'They're mostly on sea legends though, so don't be too hopeful.'

Ten minutes later, he shut the last book. 'Nothing. What about a cup of tea? I think I could manage to get that right.'

'No,' said Ruth, reaching for her coat. 'Come on. Let's get down to the library before it closes.'

The evening was calm and so cold that frost was already glittering on the pavement. Lights studded the darkness, blazing through the clear, dry air. The coast was strung with them and they shone out from houses on the high moors. The lighthouse beam traced a vivid circle, a trawler winked on the horizon and a huge, round moon hung over the sea, low enough to tip each wave with silver.

'Look at that,' said Ben, slowing down to take it all in.

Ruth hurried on. The road felt solid, but she was thinking of black, damp tunnels running under their feet and of pale shapes oozing along them.

'Hey, slow down! We've got time.'

'It's not that. I feel like I can't stand still. I mean those mines – the tunnels must run everywhere round here. Under the school, under the garage, under my house. The ground doesn't feel safe any more, Ben.'

'Oh, hell. You mean subsidence?' He caught up and slipped an arm round her, hooking his thumb into the waistline of her jeans. 'You're right about the tunnels; the whole area's riddled with them. I didn't think of that, either. In fact I've been a complete and utter pillock. Do you know what's the worst thing of all? We could've solved this weeks ago if it wasn't for me. There was that moment at Jack and Rosemary's when Jack smelled trouble, do you remember? The first night. Chances are, Jack would've known the old mining stories and if we'd talked to him . . . But no, I shut him out. And do you know why? Because I wanted to keep you to myself. Somebody really needed me for once, and I was enjoying it too much to share. Pathetic.

'I've been wrong all along the line. All that drivel about stone circles and the old magic –'

'You weren't so wrong.'

'But it's going to be a mine!'

'I know. But these stories about creatures with the power to move rock, well, perhaps it was the old earth magic you were talking about. You could've been on the right track, Ben.'

'Just heading in the wrong direction. It's all right, I'm a big boy now. I can admit it when I'm wrong. I can to you, at least. Pig-headed, you see. I get an idea in my head and, no matter how idiotic it is, I'm off. Action man. So, I drag you out in all weathers –'

'You didn't drag me. I chose to go,' said Ruth, but Ben just went on talking, walking faster with every step.

'– not listening to any of your doubts, getting you into all that trouble at school. Ah, Christ! I'm going to end up a lonely old bigot, just like my dad.'

'No, you won't!' yelled Ruth, jumping in front of him. 'You won't because you saw what he did to your mum. You won't because you care about people. And I care about you, so just shut up!'

Ben stopped. Ben stared. Ruth stared back, stunned by what had just come out of her mouth. Now Ben would realise Rosemary had told her all about his family. That censor in her head, the one which stopped her saying what she really meant, the one which was so frightened of what others would think, had just been overruled by something stronger. Time stretched, the way it used to stretch on bonfire night, in those long seconds after her dad had lit the touchpaper of a firecracker.

Ben blinked. She watched him take a deep breath and let it out. She watched his breath turn white with cold and hover in front of his face. Then he stepped forward and put his arms around her.

'Sorry,' he muttered, pushing his face into her hair. 'Sorry, sorry, sorry.'

Ruth slipped her arms around his waist, speechless with relief.

'You know,' sighed Ben, after a while, 'we've found out what's going to happen and we still can't do a thing. There must be hundreds of old tin mines in Cornwall. And even if we decide it has to be local, no

136

one's going to leave the village or close a mine because you're having nightmares and I'm losing sleep.'

'What do you mean, we can't do a thing? We carry on searching the library, we read the local papers, back issues as well. We watch the local news, listen to gossip, catch clues . . . Something might turn up. And we can try to keep ourselves safe, at least.'

Ben leaned back and looked into her face. He was smiling. 'So, you're still determined.'

'Still determined,' agreed Ruth, pushing her hands under his sweatshirt. She traced her fingers down the curve of his spine to the hollow of his back, then clasped her hands and pulled him close.

The kiss was long and slow. When it finished, Ben held her tight against him, hard enough for her to feel his heart beating.

'You know what?' she asked.

'What?' whispered Ben, kissing her neck just below the ear.

'I'm getting to like the smell of cat pee.'

Chapter Nine

On Sunday night, Ruth sat at the kitchen table long after Ben had gone, ploughing through a history of local tin mines. It was very late when she closed the book, rested her head on her arms and gazed for a moment at the photograph on the front cover. It showed a boy crouched at the top end of a sloping tunnel, shovelling rubble down the incline. One rough spar of pitch pine had been knocked in at an angle as a token roof support, but the granite hung heavy above his bent back. He was smiling straight at the camera and his teeth shone white in his dirty face.

If he'd been born a hundred years later, he'd still be at school, thought Ruth. He was local. Could've been in my form. She began to work her way through all the faces in her formclass, searching for a likeness. The kitchen was warm and quiet; quiet enough for her to hear coals shifting in the stove and ashes pattering through the grating. Somewhere around the middle of the alphabet her eyes closed and she drowsed –

– and falls

No . . .

into a pounding, roaring, spinning darkness

No . . .
  No sight
No . . .
  No breath
Hurting, choking, drowning –

Seconds later she was clinging to the kitchen table, panting and shuddering like a terrified dog. The house stood solid on its foundations. She ran to the back door, through the yard and on to the road. No lights. No sirens. The village lay quiet below her.

Back inside, she headed for her room and her radio. The national news was pretending that Britain stopped at the Home Counties and the local news was filling up its five minutes with petty theft and a burning barn.

'. . . and that's the end of the news,' chirped a relentlessly cheerful voice. 'Sounds like it's pretty quiet in Cornwall tonight, so let's liven things up with some music . . .'

Ruth shook her head. It wasn't quiet at all; it only seemed that way. Under the surface everything had changed. The beast was down there, under the ground, awake and ready.

She spent the rest of the night sitting in her wicker armchair with the radio on beside her. Twice her head nodded and twice it was as though a trapdoor opened under her feet and she plunged down into cold, wet blackness.

'Stay here,' said Ben on Monday morning. 'Stay close. You can't go to school after a night without sleep.' He held out the key to his flat, his eyes pleading.

Ruth looked away, concentrating on a stream of

oily water that was trickling from the garage gates to the gutter. 'No. If I go to school, I'll have to stay awake. It's the best thing to do.'

'Ah, but look at you. Look at you.' His voice sounded bruised. 'You can't go on like this for long.'

'I won't have to,' she said flatly. 'Something'll happen soon. It's not a dream any more. It doesn't stop when I wake up. No, it's building up all the time; it's building up now.'

'Then we'll go away until it's over. Rosemary and Jack'll have us.'

'Ben, I can't leave my mum.'

'OK, we'll take her with us. We'll tell her . . . we'll tell her . . .'

Ruth sighed. 'Stop it, Ben. I don't need this. I need you to fight.'

'I would fight if I knew what to do! It's this hanging around waiting for it –'

'I'll tell you what you do. You listen to the customers; you listen to that radio in there. You look for the slightest hint, anything that might give them away. Anything.'

'In other words,' said Ben, 'I hang around to music.'

'Ben Treseder –'

'OK, OK, I'm sorry. I'll do my best. Sure you'll be all right?'

'Yes,' said Ruth, filling her head with thoughts of Rusty.

'Still determined, then?'

'Still determined,' she said, fiercely.

Ruth struggled through the first part of the morning, trailing a gritty tiredness and flinching at every loud noise or sudden movement. No one noticed. They were busy planning Christmas parties and writing cards. Even Debbie left her alone, preferring to spend her time creating havoc with a sprig of mistletoe.

The peace did not last. Second lesson of the day was history and Mr Pugh homed in on Ruth as soon as the class was settled.

'Well? Where is it, girl?'

Ruth looked up at him. Her mind was a complete blank.

'The form and the money, girl! I said they were to be in today without fail. Without fail,' he repeated, slamming his sheaf of papers down on her head twice.

'Who else has forgotten?' he asked, turning slowly on his heel to survey the room. His shoes squeaked loudly in the silence. He turned back to Ruth, his eyes gleaming wetly, and she realised he was enjoying himself.

'Well?' He waited, breathing heavily through his nose.

'I don't know which form you mean, sir.'

'But of course!' he cried, snapping his fingers. 'You wouldn't know because you didn't get one. You were taking your little trip up the coast at the time, weren't you? Weren't you!' Slam, slam went the papers on her head.

'Yes, sir.'

'Well, now. Considering your obvious interest in local history, I am sure we will receive your full support for our little venture this Wednesday. That is, of course, presuming you have nothing else planned?'

He waited for the giggles of the class to die away

141

before he placed a piece of paper on her desk. 'Back here tomorrow, signed, or else . . .' he hissed, bringing his papers down on her head one last time.

The dictation started without warning. It was an old trick of his, but it never failed to catch them out. Ruth was forgotten in the race to open files and take notes. She sat with her head bent, blinking back the tears. She had to do it very slowly so that they did not spill over on to her cheeks, but gradually the paper swam into focus and she began to read.

Her scream exploded into the heavy classroom air. Several of the class yelped softly, like echoes. They yelped again when her chair crashed to the ground. She headed for the front and Mr Pugh jumped behind his desk, letting his notes fall to the floor with a dry rustle. Then she was out of the room and running down the corridor. Behind her, Mr Pugh clawed at his tight collar and the whole class sat transfixed, staring at the open door.

'She's here again.'

Ben slid out from under the Austin and scrambled to his feet. 'What?' he said, staring at his boss.

'Your girl. In the office. She's –' he paused, considering his options, '– upset. We'll call it your tea break then, shall we?' he yelled as Ben turned and raced for the door.

She must have been running hard. She was leaning over the swivel chair with her hand pressed to her side, gasping for air.

'What is it?' asked Ben, kicking shut the office door. 'What? Are you hurt?'

Ruth tried to speak but her breath wailed in her throat. She shook her head.

'What then? Has it happened? Not the school?'

She shook her head again and held out a crumpled piece of paper. It was a typed letter. Ben smoothed it out on the desk and began to read.

Dear Parent/Guardian,

A substantial amount of our fourth-year history option will be devoted to local topics in the Spring term and, by way of an appetiser, we are hoping to end this term with an outing.

You may know that a disused cliffside tin mine, only a few miles from the school, has been turned into an interesting showpiece.

Briefly, it consists of a purpose-built complex containing a museum, shop and cafeteria, a selection of restored surface buildings, and an underground reconstruction of a nineteenth-century tin mine, housed in the passages of the original mine.

The company have assured us that the development has undergone rigorous checks and is completely safe –

Ben stopped reading and turned back to Ruth. The shock had left her face and her breathing was nearly back to normal.

'When?' he asked.

'Wednesday.'

'Two days; you were right about it happening soon. I know the place,' he added, swinging himself up on to the desk and trapping his shaking hands under his thighs. 'I remember when that company bought it a couple of years ago. The village thought there might be jobs if they were opening up the mine again, but everyone lost interest when they heard it was going to be a museum. I didn't even know it had opened.'

'Only just. It says there we'll be among the first visitors.'

'A school party . . .' breathed Ben, and shivered.

'Where is it, this mine?'

'Not far from that engine house where Rusty . . .'

'Where Rusty died?'

Ben nodded. 'You can't see it until you're almost on top of it because it's hidden by a dip in the cliffs. Some of the tunnels must run right under the engine house and link up with those openings in the cliffs.'

Ruth sighed. 'I had a feeling it would be there.' She walked over and leaned up against the desk, between Ben's dangling legs. He pulled her close to his chest, resting his chin on the top of her head. 'All right?' he asked.

'Yes, I'm all right. It was a shock, finding out like that, but now, well, we've got a time and a place. Something to work on. Perhaps we can beat this after all.'

'We've got a lot of persuading to do.'

'I know. What if I go back to the school and you see what you can do at the mining museum?'

'I'll go now,' said Ben, his face lighting up at the prospect of action. 'If I take my bike, I'll be there in half an hour. Come on.'

'Hoy! Where d'you think you're going?'

'Early lunch, Mr Hambley,' called Ben, without breaking his stride.

'What about this Austin?'

'I'll make it up to you!' yelled Ben, swinging into the saddle.

'Now, just one minute –!'

144

'See you tonight,' whispered Ben and pedalled away, his legs pumping hard to get some speed out of the heavy old bike.

Ruth watched him out of sight, then forced herself to turn and climb the hill back to school.

'That's enough!' shouted Mr Pugh, as soon as he understood. 'That is enough! There will be no accident, do you hear me, girl? There will be no disaster, because you are a liar!' He was so angry, he did a little hopping dance on Mrs Sheraton's rose-pink carpet. 'The headmistress and I have no time for lies, especially when they have been invented to justify the sort of disruptive behaviour I would expect from an inner-city delinquent –'

'Thank you, Mr Pugh,' said Mrs Sheraton, looking with distaste at the tiny bubbles of spit he had sprayed across her desk. 'I'm sorry to have taken up so much of your lunch hour.'

Ruth, watching the dismissal, felt hope begin to stir.

'Do sit down, dear,' said Mrs Sheraton when they were alone. 'Now,' she smiled, pulling a tissue from the box and wiping down her desk, 'do you think you can tell me?'

Gratefully, Ruth launched into her story again. When she finished, the smile had gone.

'Very well, Ruth,' said Mrs Sheraton, lighting up a cigarette. 'I had hoped you would confide in me but I was wrong. You leave me no option but to take things further. That is all, for now.'

Ruth tried Mr Edwards next. 'Oh dear,' he said. 'It all sounds, ah, very alarming. What can we do?' He

145

searched the walls of the quiet corridor as though the answer might be written there. Ruth held her breath.

'Um, can you, ah, leave it with me? I'll have a chat with all concerned and see what I can do.'

'Oh, thank you, sir.'

'No promises, though –' he said, then stopped with his mouth open, staring over her right shoulder. A sweaty blush stained his cheeks.

'Now, look here,' he blustered, shifting his eyes back to Ruth. 'I think I've heard enough of this, um, of this nonsense. It's, ah, it's really not on, you know . . .'

Ruth turned round and there was Mr Pugh, glowering from the staffroom doorway. She turned back to Mr Edwards but he was gazing at Mr Pugh like a spaniel. Ruth walked away without another word and headed for the formroom.

'Let me get this straight. We all have to tell old Puke that we don't want a day away from this dump, because you and that wally from the garage think some little white men are going to turn nasty.' Debbie looked around the group, her expression unreadable, then said, 'You sure those little white men weren't wearing little white coats?'

'I'm telling you, I was having nightmares about this trip long before any of us knew about it!' shouted Ruth and the laughter stopped. 'Look, haven't you ever known what was going to happen? Known what someone was about to say? What about recognising a place you've never been to before? Or thinking about someone and the next minute they phone up? It's not so unusual, is it?'

For three seconds no one spoke. The fluorescent

lights buzzed in the silence. Then they began to talk; not to her, but to one another. Ruth crossed her fingers.

'My grandma says she felt it when my grandad was killed in France. She knew it before the telegram arrived –'

'My aunt phoned my mum in the middle of the night and told her to check the kitchen and someone had left the grill on –'

'Yeah, I was reading something about dreams –'

'I don't believe this!' shrieked Debbie. 'Listen to you!'

'Come on, then,' said Spaghetti-hair, with a hint of a challenge, 'tell us what you think.'

Debbie's answer could not have been better chosen to destroy the mood. Turning round, she lifted her skirt and made a loud farting noise.

'And that was it,' said Ruth that evening. 'They all just collapsed.'

'Typical Debbie,' said Ben. 'And typical Sheraton. Makes me feel sorry for Pugh. Almost.'

'You are joking?'

'No, really. She sets him up as the tough guy and he doesn't even know it. She just wheels him in, switches him on to do his bit, then wheels him right out again.'

'Tough guy?' asked Ruth, putting two mugs of tea on the table. 'What are you talking about?'

'You know, your interview with Sheraton. It's an old police trick. The tough guy gives you a hard time, then he leaves the room and the nice guy takes over. Tea and sympathy. You're supposed to be so grateful, you confess everything.'

'So that's why she turned cold on me. She thought I was holding something back.' Ruth shook her head. 'I didn't have a clue what she was up to.'

'Neither did I when she tried it on me, that day I told them I was leaving. I only figured it out afterwards.' He stared down into his mug, remembering.

'I suppose they wouldn't listen at the mine, either?'

'They did to start with. When I told them at reception that I'd come from the village with a problem, they phoned the manager and I got straight in to see him. I think they're under orders to be kind to the locals. It sort of went downhill after I told him.'

'What did he say?'

'He said I was a fool if I thought he was going to close the place down after his company had just spent two years pouring money down the shaft.'

'Oh.'

'Do you want to hear the rest? I'll just give you the edited highlights. I said I would go and give the story to the *Mercury*. He said the editor was his brother-in-law. I asked him if he had any relatives running the local radio station. He said no, but the company had just paid a whole lot of money for a series of radio adverts. I called him something very rude. He told me to get out before he called site security.'

'Oh,' said Ruth again.

Ben came and squatted by her chair, resting his hands on her thighs and looking up into her face. 'Well, we tried,' he said.

'We tried? What do you mean, we tried? We can't stop now.'

Ben straightened up, scowling. 'I can. I could lose my job if I take any more time off without notice. And that means I lose my flat too. Besides, what else can we do?'

'Not much of a fighter, are you? Giving up just because the odds are against you. And if that sounds familiar, you said it to me the first time we met.'

'This is different.'

'How?'

'It just is.'

'How? How is it different? People still might die.'

Ben jumped to his feet and his chair clattered away over the stone floor. 'Yes, but it won't be you!' he yelled, thumping the kitchen table. 'It won't be you, it won't be your mum and it won't be me. There. It may not be very pretty but it is honest. And you haven't answered me yet. What else can we do?'

'I know what I'm going to do,' shouted Ruth, jumping up to face him. 'I'm going on that trip.'

She sat down again, looking startled. Ben stared.

'Come on, Ruth. You didn't mean that. It's the lack of sleep . . .'

'No, I think I did mean it,' said Ruth and felt a sweet calm spread through her body like warm honey. 'It's the only thing left to do.'

After a few stunned seconds, Ben leaned across the table, thrusting his face into hers. 'What are you planning to do? Hold up the roof when it starts to cave in? Stop the water from rising? This is no time for a Superwoman fantasy.'

'I'm just going to be there, expecting something to go wrong. It might make all the difference.'

Ben shook his head, incredulous.

'It might, Ben. Anyway, I've got to try, otherwise everything I've been through the last few months –'

'Oh,' said Ben, sinking back into his chair, 'now I

see what it is. Ruth, I know how much you must want to hit back after what happened to Rusty, but –'

'No. You're wrong. It's more than that. I told you what Edwards did today, saying he would help me until he realised Pugh was listening. That's exactly what I did to you in front of Debbie, remember? Well, I don't want to reach his age and still be a spaniel.'

'If you go down that mine, you might not reach his age, full stop!'

'I know it'll be risky, but you have to take risks when you're fighting for the important things. You have to.'

'Ruth,' said Ben carefully, 'if you're doing this to prove something to me, you don't have to. I know you've changed.'

'It's not for you. Not like that, anyway. If it was, then I'd still just be trying to please someone else, wouldn't I?'

Ben got up and marched across the room until he ran up against the kitchen sink. He stood in silence for a moment, staring out into the dark backyard. 'That lot at the school are going to have a fine time,' he said, keeping his back to Ruth. 'What'll they say when you tell them you're going after all? What'll they think?'

'Oh, Ben. Is that the only argument you've got left? I bet you can't look me in the eye and say that.'

Ben turned round and looked at her, his face full of an angry sorrow. Then he sighed and looked down at the floor, letting himself slump backwards to rest against the sink. 'OK, I give in. We'll both go.'

'But – it's a school trip –'

'The museum's open to everyone. I'll just buy a

ticket and follow you down. No problem as long as the manager isn't around. That reminds me –' Ben walked over to the chair where he had left his coat and picked up a long roll of paper that was propped up against it. 'When I left, his secretary wasn't in her office, so I nicked this. There were five or six of them in a sort of umbrella stand so they shouldn't miss one.'

He put it at the edge of the table and unrolled the first section, holding it in place with their empty mugs. Ruth stared at the tangle of lines for a few seconds, then suddenly understood.

'It's a plan of the mine!'

'Yeah. I was so mad, I just walked out of the building with it stuck under my arm. You see, they've marked the reconstruction in green and here are all the tunnels that link up to it. Those yellow ones are safe and the red ones are dangerous or blocked.'

'But, this is great, Ben! If we can learn all the ways out of there –'

'It'll be complicated, though. This is just one cross-section. This roll is full of them, showing all the different levels and cross-cuts –'

'Shut up,' said Ruth, sliding herself between Ben and the table. 'We can do it. But first . . .'

It was Ben who broke the kiss. 'Cut it out,' he whispered. 'Your mum might walk in.'

'She won't. She'll stay away from me tonight. Sheraton phoned again.'

'Oh. Upset, was she?'

'She doesn't know how she'll face her customers tomorrow after their kids have told them all about it. She thinks I'm doing it to force her into moving back to Coventry. You know, she's going to be so pleased

151

when I tell her I've decided to go on the trip. Crazy, isn't it? Perhaps I'll really cheer her up and tell her it was just a joke that got out of hand.'

Ben gazed over her shoulder at the plan. 'I wish it was,' he said.

That night, Ruth was so desperate for rest, she risked a sleeping tablet, hoping the drug would block out the beast. It worked. She managed four hours of uneasy sleep before the effect wore off and the trapdoor opened.

She woke a few seconds later, gasping for breath. In the very same instant, a group of roosting seagulls all flew into the dark air together, circling the cliffs in a squawking panic. The overhang where they were perching had moved; shuddering and groaning as though it would tear itself away from the cliff. It was quiet now and apparently steady against the heaving shoulder of the sea, but the seagulls did not return.

Chapter Ten

Ruth started at one end of the shop and worked her way round the shelves. She took two strong nylon washing-lines, a torch and spare batteries, three rolls of crêpe bandage and four large bars of chocolate. The lights came on as she was fastening her rucksack.

'Well, look at you! Hiking boots and everything. Mind you, that jacket's seen better days and haven't you got some smarter cords?'

'Mum, it's not a fashion show. They said to wear warm clothes and this jacket's padded.'

'Oh well, if they told you to. Rucksack as well? What's in there?'

'History file. And sandwiches. And, um, I'd better go. We're supposed to be at the crossroads by nine to catch the coast-road bus.'

'Right, well enjoy your trip, dear. And Ruthie? You will be good, won't you? Make an effort?'

'Yes, Mum.'

Mrs Davis smiled and offered her cheek. Ruth touched her lips to the soft skin and breathed in the scent of face powder.

'Mum –'

'Yes, dear?'

'Mum –'

But the bread van was pulling up outside and soon the driver would be rattling at the shop door. 'Just – take care.'

'Gather round,' ordered Mr Pugh, unnecessarily. With the exception of Ruth, the whole history group was trying to find shelter under the eaves of the ticket office, but the museum complex was in a small valley that sloped down to a dip in the cliffs, and it was like standing at the end of a wind tunnel. Each blast was icy cold and spiked with rain.

Ruth stood apart, scanning the site. Mr Pugh ignored her, as he had done since she arrived at the crossroads, and the rest of the group followed his cue. She spotted the bike first, chained to the drainpipe of the cafeteria. Then a white smudge of a face behind one of the steamed-up windows nodded and raised its cup to her. Ruth smiled and turned back to the group.

'In view of the worsening weather,' Mr Pugh was saying, 'we shall look at the old surface buildings first, then we can spend the rest of the day indoors.'

'Oh, sir,' said Debbie, looking longingly at the lights of the cafeteria, 'can't we take the worksheets and split up? That's what Mrs Beddows did when we went to –'

'I am not Mrs Beddows. Now, follow me.'

Ruth held back for a moment, staring down the valley at a large shed that looked as though it had been rammed into the base of the hill. Inside that shed was the entrance to the mine. She swallowed, trying to find some saliva, but her tongue lay in her mouth like a wad of cotton wool. She turned to check that Ben had left the cafeteria, before hurrying down the path after the others.

Near the cliff edge, the earth fell away in wide, sweeping terraces, covered in red clay and dotted with grey crumbling mine buildings. Streams of red water ran down the terraces and plummeted over the edge to stain the sea. Staves of rotting wood and spars of rusty iron lay everywhere. The place had the raw, weeping look of a neglected wound. The wind roared and the first of a bank of storm clouds mushroomed overhead, but Mr Pugh still tried to give a lecture on the points of interest. The group huddled miserably.

Ruth concentrated on searching the skyline back from the mine entrance until she spotted the top of an engine-house chimney that marked the original mine shaft. This was the place where Rusty had died. The cliff face below the engine house was in full view and she could see the dark holes that Ben had called the Old Men's Workings. Under the holes, the cliff face had worn away, leaving a massive overhang poised above the sea. Huge waves crashed against the overhang and spray filled the air.

Just then, something white moved at the edge of her vision. She turned. A few loose stones skittered down one of the terraces. Nothing else. She let the breath go from her lungs, relaxed her shoulders and a pale hand slid over the edge of the path like an eel, grabbing for her ankle.

Ruth jumped away, landed on the opposite side of the path, scurried back to the middle and stopped. There was nowhere to go. She was stuck on a narrow strip of concrete with muddy terraces all around her. The hand appeared again, waved madly and became a white plastic bag caught on a piece of wood. Ruth groaned and stared desperately at Mr Pugh, but he showed no signs of finishing the lecture.

'Jumpy, aren't we?' muttered Debbie. 'Or is it a new sort of dance?'

'Shut it, Pascoe,' growled Barry Curnow unexpectedly, taking in Ruth's face.

It began to rain. Not the isolated splutters that had been carried in the wind all morning, but a heavy, hard downpour.

'Inside!' ordered Mr Pugh and the group broke up and ran towards the shed at the mine entrance, leaving him gasping along behind.

The back wall of the shed was the valleyside and two pairs of double doors were set into the granite. One pair was marked NO ENTRY and a blackboard was propped against the other pair, with the words 'Next opening 10.00' chalked across it.

'You nearly missed it,' said the young attendant, looking at his watch. 'School trip, is it? Where's your teacher?'

At that moment, Mr Pugh staggered in and stood there, wheezing and dripping, with his black woolly hat pulled down low over his ears.

'Good morning, sir,' said the attendant, straight-faced as the class collapsed around him. 'How many in your party, including yourself?'

'Eleven. I mean twelve,' gasped Mr Pugh, sliding a glance over Ruth and away again.

'OK, folks,' said the attendant, squatting down to write the number on the board. 'Three points. First, we always know how many visitors are in the mine. It takes half an hour to go round at a slow walk, so if you're not all back here within forty-five minutes, we send someone down to make sure you're all right.

'Second, it's a circular route, so you can't lose your way. Just stay on the boardwalks and you can only end up back here.

'Third, you need to wear one of these.' He reached into the plastic bin beside him and brought out a yellow hard hat. 'Apart from making them safe, we've left the passages as they were and the roof is a bit low in places. Please don't use the helmet lamps. We've installed a good lighting system, so they're only for emergencies. Right, that's the boring bit over. Here we go . . .'

He pushed open the doors. There was a hush as the group stared down the bland length of a well-lit, concrete corridor. Then they all started talking at once, reaching for helmets and fighting to be at the front.

'Stop!' howled Mr Pugh, his voice back to full strength. 'Curnow! You wait there, boy. I'll lead the way.'

The group fell in behind him, giggling and pushing, but Ruth waited just inside the corridor until Ben came through the outer doors.

'Sorry, mate,' said the attendant, catching sight of him. 'You'll have to wait for the next one now.'

'But they've only just started. I can catch them up –'

'Sorry. Once the number's on the board, no one else goes in. Safety regulations.' He slammed the first door and pushed home the bolts.

'No, wait!' yelled Ruth, as the second door began to close. 'He's with us.'

The attendant paused, still holding the door half shut. 'I dunno. Your teacher said twelve.'

'Yes, but – Mr Pugh thought he wasn't coming –'

'– I slept in, missed the bus. But I hitched a lift –'

'Well . . .'

'Go on,' pleaded Ruth. 'He'll get into a lot of trouble if he misses it.'

'All right,' sighed the attendant. 'In you go.' He rubbed out the number chalked on the board and wrote in the new one. 'Thirteen. Unlucky for some,' he said, and winked at them before closing the second door and shutting them in the corridor.

'Ben! You didn't get a helmet.'

'No time now,' said Ben, grimly. 'Get after them. I'll be right behind you.'

Ruth squared her shoulders and plunged into the mine.

The rest of the group had turned left at the end of the corridor and disappeared down a flight of steps. At the bottom of the steps, the concrete ran out and granite took over. Ruth knew from the stolen plans that they were in the main tramming level. 'The busiest highway of the mine,' her library book had said. 'Most of the ore from other levels and cross-cuts was brought here and taken in waggons to the shaft.'

Ruth had imagined something like a subway but there was nothing smooth and regular about this tunnel. It had been hacked out with picks and blasted by explosives. The rock face was pitted with random holes and hollows where miners had spotted the rusty red of tin and stopped to gouge it out. In some places the tunnel was so narrow, its sides carried a shoulder-high strip of rock worn smooth as glass by passing waggon rims. In other places, it was as wide and high as her front room.

All the tunnels that opened on to this one had been

sealed with steel doors, but there were still burrow-
ings and crevices too deep for the lights to penetrate.
Ruth scurried past them, all her senses on the alert.
She heard nothing but her own boots thudding softly
on the boardwalk. The air was warm and musty, with
a faint tang of new-cut wood, but that was all.

The others were gathered round a huge old wooden
door propped up against the side of the tunnel and she
hurried to catch up.

'Down here, madam, you stay with us,' hissed Mr
Pugh when she reached them.

'Yes, sir,' muttered Ruth, her eyes darting everywhere.

'All right,' continued Mr Pugh, turning back to the
exhibit. 'These doors were put in to help the air
pumps do their work. Boys over ten worked with
their fathers below surface, and the younger ones had
to open and shut these doors when the waggons came
through. Good reason to do your job properly, don't
you think? Making sure your dad gets enough fresh
air to stay alive?'

'Depends on who your dad is,' whispered Debbie,
making Spaghetti-hair snigger behind her hand.

Ruth stared at the door, seeing all the young boys
who had spent their days sitting next to it, wide-eyed
in the dusty dark. Then Mr Pugh moved them on,
past displays of old carbide lamps and mining tools,
to a place where two openings were cut low in the
rock, one on each side of the tunnel. They were
shaped like rough letterboxes and each was about ten
yards long.

'You see how the miners worked?' said Mr Pugh.
'They just followed the tin wherever they found it. It
was called stoping. They would work on their knees

rather than drill away waste rock, as you can see from this stope.'

Ruth forced herself to crouch down and peer in, ready to jump up and run at the slightest movement. The stope slid away into darkness on either side, wide and shallow like a plate. Its low roof was propped up with timbers almost as thick as they were high.

It was empty, apart from Barry Curnow, who had crawled part way in. 'Oh wow!' he called. 'It's just like that bit in *Indiana Jones* . . .'

He crawled even further in and tried an experimental yodel. Ruth held her breath until he backed out again. Tracey Penrose was gazing dreamily up into the roof, her thin, white legs looking fragile against the black opening. Ruth imagined something sliding from the stope, grabbing Tracey by the ankles and dragging her in under the lip of rock. Sweat gathered damply in the palms of her hands.

At last Mr Pugh called them together and they walked on down the tunnel, past floodlit sections of wall that were marbled with white quartz stringers or the bright glitter of fool's gold. Fifty yards on, the tunnel was blocked by a steel door set in concrete and another flight of steps led down to the right.

'Pay attention, now. We're leaving the tramming level here and going into a cross-cut. Who can tell me what that is?'

Everyone looked at the walls, the roof or their feet.

'Come on! We learnt about the structure of a mine only yesterday . . . All right, I'll remind you. A cross-cut is an exploratory tunnel; they were looking for more tin. And it's so low and narrow because . . . ?'

'Hard rock mining, sir.'

'And . . . ?'

'It's expensive to drill, sir.'

'Well done, Tracey. On we go.'

The staircase narrowed steadily, forcing them into single file. When they reached the bottom, the taller ones had to stoop to get into the cross-cut. It was a tiny tunnel, just wide enough to turn around in. The lights had been recessed into the wall, but they were close enough for Ruth to feel their faint heat on her face as she passed. She tried to take calm breaths of the warm, stale air, but just knowing that she could not spread her arms without meeting rock made her want to run. Please, not here . . . not here, she begged.

Someone cursed as his helmet cracked against the roof. It was strangely muffled and without echo, as though he was talking with his head in a box. Barry Curnow began to sing 'Keep right on to the end of the road,' but he soon tailed off. The granite seemed to eat sound. They shuffled on, subdued.

Then Mr Pugh shouted from the front and the word came back, 'More stairs, going down . . . More stairs going down. He says it opens out at the bottom . . . it opens out . . .'

Ruth heard the message coming down the line and turned to give Ben a thumbs-up sign, but he was not there. The cross-cut was empty. Then she remembered. Sitting in her kitchen the night before, Ben had pointed to the plan, tracing the length of the cross-cut with his finger. 'That's a nasty little one. I'm going to wait at the top here and give you all time to go through before I go in.'

'Good idea,' she had said. 'Then you can get help if anything happens in there.'

It had all sounded very sensible in her kitchen but

161

now, this was the first time Ben had been out of her sight, and she hated it. For two seconds, Ruth was undecided, then she turned and hurried after Debbie.

The company had blasted a way through the floor of the cross-cut and continued down at a forty-five degree angle until they had breached the side wall of a deeper level. Then they had put in steps and re-inforced the stairwell with arches of steel. Ruth stood on the top step and peered across at the interrupted cross-cut. The gap was too wide for even the most foolhardy tourist to jump across, so the opening had not been sealed off. It hung at the top of the stairwell like a blackened portrait.

She swallowed and edged down the stairs, craning her neck to keep the opening above in sight as long as she could. She took the last steps in one jump, shot out into the level and crashed against the far wall. Spinning around, she stared up into the stairwell. Nothing.

Debbie giggled. 'What's after us now?' she sneered and flounced off after the others.

Ruth turned to follow, glanced once more up the stairs and there they were, standing in a pale line, grinning.

'Look out!' she screamed. An instant later the rock beneath her feet humped itself upwards and flowed forward in a rippling movement like a snake. Every-one struggled to keep their feet in a surprised, silent dance, but they were flicked to the ground. The whole tunnel began to shake as a rumble echoed through the mine, building to a deep and terrible roar.

The site manager was looking straight at the old engine-house chimney when it began to crumble. He had just turned his swivel chair to the window and settled back with a mid-morning coffee to survey the development. He watched with growing horror as the whole overhang broke away from the cliff and crashed into the sea, taking the engine house with it.

Sea water boiled up the little valley as far as the pathways, sucking at the heels of fleeing visitors. The ground shuddered and a cloud of dust belched from the entrance to the show mine. The attendant stumbled from the shed seconds before it fell on to its side and folded up.

People in the cafeteria at the top of the valley were the last to panic. At first they were merely puzzled or annoyed as their drinks slopped over the top of the plastic cups. When the rumbling started, some looked out at the sky, expecting to see low-flying Air Force jets. A few screamed when a crack sliced across the picture window, but they didn't start to fight and push their way out until they saw the first of a stream of terrified people running back up for the gates.

The manager was running the other way: down the valley to the show-mine attendant. 'How many?' he shrieked. 'How many down there?'

'Thirteen,' spluttered the attendant and he bent double to cough up more dust. 'Thirteen . . . unlucky for some . . .' He gave an hysterical hoot. 'School party . . .'

'Oh, my God.' The manager's face turned the colour of Cheshire cheese. He gazed around wildly and sighed with relief when he spotted the approaching security guard. 'Here's Bill. He'll know what to do. He used to work here before.'

'I've called the lads out,' said Bill. 'They'll be here soon.'

'The lads?'

'The rescue team,' said Bill, trying to steady his voice. 'From when she was a real mine.'

'Oh, yes. What do you think, Bill? What happened?'

'Lots of dust. That means rock falls in the mine, probably set off by that cliff coming down. Plenty of them as well, to cause all that quaking above ground. She's a big one.'

'Bill, there are kids down there. What – what are their chances?'

The old miner just shook his head.

Chapter Eleven

Ruth opened her eyes. The lights still shone in a flickering, indecisive way, but the air was so choked with dust, it was hard to see. She took a breath to shout and began to cough instead. Her mouth was full of grit. She swallowed hard, held her breath and listened. There were clunks and light, dry patterings as small rocks and pebbles fell.

Someone coughed.

Someone sobbed.

Ruth sat up. There was a throbbing lump on the side of her jaw but otherwise the helmet and padded jacket had cushioned her fall. She eased on to her hands and knees and crawled through the settling dust towards the sounds. She found the others, still lined up in the order they had been walking, like a row of fallen dominoes. Most people were beginning to get to their feet, but Tracey Penrose was curled in a ball, crying, and Barry Curnow was on his hands and knees being very sick. At the head of the line, Mr Pugh was lying slumped against the wall. He was sucking in harsh, gasping breaths and staring dazedly at the rock fall that blocked the tunnel a few yards in front of him. Bright blood streaked the dusty grey of his face.

Ruth staggered to her feet, turned and squinted back down the tunnel. There was no sign of Ben.

Oh, God – not him . . . She began to stumble towards the stairs, but Debbie blocked her way.

'I don't know how you did this, but you'll be sorry –'

'Get out of my way!' yelled Ruth, with such violence that Debbie fell back.

The staircase was deserted; the creatures had gone. Ruth forced herself to walk up to the top, testing each step. Then she turned, heart pounding, and stared into the black hole above her head. Nothing. She turned away, feeling the skin crawl on her neck, and plunged back along the narrow cross-cut. On she went at a crouching run until she reached the steps leading up to the tramming level. Then she stopped. She had to. The steps had disappeared under a heap of shattered rock.

'Ben! Ben, can you hear me?'

There was no answer. Ruth began to cry. Picking up a lump of granite, she pounded against the wall of the cross-cut. One, two, three. Then again: one, two, three. She pressed her ear to the wall and listened, but she was sobbing too hard to hear anything else.

Bending down, she began to pull at a chunk of rock. The whole pile shifted, sending boulders thundering along the cross-cut behind her. Ruth curled up against the wall until the rockfall settled again, then she climbed to her feet and stood, waiting for her knees to stop wobbling.

Idiot! He's gone for help, that's all. He knows he can't get through to us so he's gone for help. Yes. Ruth nodded emphatically, then turned and hurried back to the others.

Mr Pugh was still leaning against the wall with blood pulsing from a deep gash in his scalp, but his eyes were sharp and beady again. He moved his head, painfully, to look at her.

'Where've you been, girl?'

'Back along the cross-cut, sir. It's completely blocked at the other end.'

'How will we get out?' quavered Tracey. She began to cry again and several others joined her.

'Quiet!' grated Mr Pugh. 'Curnow, go and check.'

'But, sir –' Ruth began.

'I said quiet!' Mr Pugh glared at Ruth. 'Go on, Curnow.'

They waited in silence until Barry came panting back.

'She's right, sir. There's a rockfall where the upper stairs were.'

'I see. Then we simply wait for rescue. They know we're down here.' He pressed a folded handkerchief to the cut on his head and eased the hard hat back into place. 'Now, help me up. They may want to clear a way through this fall.'

They straggled back to the round steel door that sealed the tunnel just beyond the stairs to the cross-cut. Tracey was still sobbing and Mr Pugh patted her on the shoulder, awkwardly.

'Now come on, girl. No one's been badly hurt and we'll be out of here soon. In the meantime I want everyone to get out any food or drink you've brought along; we all need something to take away the taste of this dust.'

'Why not?' said Barry. 'Lovely spot for a picnic.'

It was a feeble joke but it raised a laugh and took some of the tension from the air. Slowly, they settled

167

down to passing round cans of drink and sandwiches, glad of something to do. They even began to chat, but no one spoke to Ruth. No one wanted to talk about dreams that came true. No one would even look her in the eye, except Debbie, who glared. Ruth was sharing a space the size of a small kitchen with eleven other people, and she had never felt so alone.

I wish Alison was here, she thought. Alison would talk to me. But scientists didn't go on history trips; scientists stayed warm and safe in their laboratories. Ruth bent over her rucksack and pulled out the four bars of chocolate that she had taken from the shop that morning. As she leaned forward to put them on the boardwalk next to a carefully packed sandwich box, the rich smell of homemade fruit cake took her by surprise. She stared at the neat foil parcels, transfixed with a sudden longing for her mother and the way things used to be. When I get out of here, we'll make it better, Mum, she vowed, blinking back the tears.

'That's Carol's lunchbox, so keep off,' hissed Debbie and Ruth jumped back, startled. She turned away from Debbie's giggle, leaned one hand against the wall and began to read a notice on that steel door. 'You are now below sea level,' it said, in bright scarlet print. 'Beyond this door, the passage extends for more than a mile beneath the sea-bed. Miners claimed that, on rough days, they could hear pebbles being dragged to and fro above their heads –'

Ruth paused to wipe her wet hand on her cords and froze, staring at the place where her hand had rested. A thin film of water was flowing down the wall from the side of the steel door. She licked her finger. *Salt.*

She turned again to face the others. They were

sitting just like the faceless people in her dreams. Calm; unsuspecting; waiting for rescue. Ruth watched with a growing sense of unreality as Carol Yelland peeled a hard-boiled egg and Barry Curnow balanced an empty Coke can on his nose. She shook her head and walked very carefully over to Mr Pugh, who was sitting slightly apart from the rest.

'Sir?' she whispered, squatting down next to him. 'Sir, we can't stay here. It's dangerous.'

He turned and frowned at her in the flickering light. Then he grabbed her arm, pulled her towards him and spat the words into her face. 'If you start a panic now, I'll have you punished so severely when we get out –'

'Sir! We won't get out if we wait here,' Ruth interrupted. 'This tunnel, the part that goes out under the sea, I think it's caved in. There's sea water leaking in all around that steel door and I don't know how long it'll hold. If it floods in here – oh, sir, we've got to climb, as high as we can.'

For a long moment Mr Pugh stared into her face, his mouth working. Then he let go of her arm. 'All right. Show me.'

It happened as she was helping him to his feet. The whole passage jarred, a crack sliced its way along the wall and, just before the lights went out, Ruth saw the steel door buckle inwards as though a giant fist had slammed into it.

Then they were scrambling and falling in complete darkness with ice-cold water beating down on them. Ruth crashed back against the wall and stayed there, huddled against the freezing tide, too shocked to move. One tiny light appeared in front of her, bobbing in the darkness.

'Helmet lamps! Put on your helmet lamps!' screamed Mr Pugh, his voice thin and high against the hissing roar of the water. Ruth fumbled at her helmet and found the switch. Other lights came on in ones and twos until it was bright enough to see again. The door still held, but it had been dented out of shape and a high-powered jet of water was shooting from a gap at the top. The rockfall further down the tunnel was acting as a dam and water was already rising above the level of the boardwalk.

'Stairs!' ordered Mr Pugh.

Minutes later, they were crammed together, three to a step, wet and shivering, their white faces turned up to Ruth and Mr Pugh as they stood together at the top.

'That's the only way,' said Ruth, pointing to the dark hole at the top of the stairwell. 'If we can get into there and if it's not blocked, we can get through to a level that leads to the old mine shaft. We can climb the shaft, if it's clear, because it goes up at an angle.'

'A lot of ifs,' said Mr Pugh. 'But you're right. We can't stay here.' He looked at the side wall, judging the distances between each steel girder, searching for ledges. 'Daniels!' he rapped, singling out the tallest, most powerful boy in the group. 'Think you could climb that?'

'I think so, sir.'

'Good. If we make some sort of a rope out of belts and clothes –'

'I've got some rope, sir,' said Ruth, bringing the washing-lines from her rucksack and holding them out to him. For a split second their eyes locked, then

170

he accepted the rope without comment, as he had accepted her knowledge of the mine.

Mark Daniels climbed. Wedging his feet between girder and rock, feeling for the slightest handhold, he made his slow way across the side wall, while the others held their breath beneath him. At last he hoisted himself over the lip of the further stretch of cross-cut. He caught the washing-line at the third throw and lowered the looped end down to Mr Pugh. Then he wrapped the slack round and round his waist and braced his feet against the sides of the cross-cut.

'Ready, sir,' he said, taking a firm grip on the line.

'I'll go first,' said Debbie, pushing her way up to the top step. 'I'm the smallest. Let me go first!'

'No, I'm the smallest,' whimpered Tracey, trying to squeeze to the front.

'Me! Me!'

'No, let me!'

They all began to push and struggle. Carol Yelland screamed as she went down and someone trod on her hand. Debbie began jumping to reach the swinging clothes-line.

'Quiet!' roared Mr Pugh. 'Stand still!' And they did. He moved in fast, knowing he only had seconds before the clamour started up again. 'Right. Ruth goes first, with the second rope tied round her waist. She gives three tugs on the line when she's through. That way we'll know how long the tunnel is and the rest of you will have a guide-line.'

On he went, talking all the time, controlling the whole thing as though he was taking a gym class. His matter-of-fact discipline made poor soil for panic to grow in and in two minutes he had them into line.

171

'Ready, girl?' he asked, turning back to Ruth. She looked up at the dark tunnel, clenched her fists and nodded.

They lifted her as high as they could and Mark hauled her the rest of the way, with the nylon loop biting into her armpits. She clambered to her feet and stared into the blackness.

'Go on!' shouted Mr Pugh from below.

'Doesn't believe in asking for volunteers, does he?' muttered Mark, inspecting the rope burns on his hands.

'Hurry, girl!'

Ruth walked into the cross-cut. Her lamp beam made crazy patterns over the rough walls and the air was heavy with the stink of stagnant water. Noises from the stairwell faded rapidly and soon the only sounds were her frightened breathing and the crunch of her boots on the granite floor. She was trying very hard not to think about the creatures but, every few yards, she turned and probed the darkness with her lamp beam. The line around her waist tugged gently as she walked and she tried to keep a picture of the white rope linking her to the others.

Gradually, the ground began to slope upwards and the roof got lower until she was struggling up the incline at a crouch. Cramp tied knots in her thigh muscles but the thought of the water below and the granite two inches from her back forced her on. The gap grew smaller still and her crouch became a crawl. Soon she was sobbing with fear and effort. The need to stand up was overwhelming.

Still, the roof got lower and the walls closed in. Ruth stopped. Her breath wailed in her throat. She tried to sit up to loosen her jacket at the neck but her helmet clanged against rock. She tried to twist round to see behind her but the tunnel was too narrow. When she lifted her head to peer over her shoulder, her helmet scraped along the roof.

Ruth pushed forward another few yards, then stopped again, staring in horror at what she saw in her lamp beam. The roof dipped even further.

I'm going to have to squirm. I'm going to have to squirm into that little gap and push myself along the ground and will I ever, ever come out the other side? Will I ever, ever get out? I'm so far under the ground and the rock above me, all the weight of the rock above me . . . Oh, the rock and the water and the . . .

Ruth deliberately turned her head and sank her teeth into her arm. While the pain was still fierce, she began to chant, 'One two is two, two twos are four, three twos are six,' and as she chanted, she began to move, pushing herself forward inch by inch.

She had reached the seven-times table when, without warning, her head was clear of the rock. Then she could spread her arms. Slowly, she eased from the end of the cross-cut and dropped to the ground in a tunnel.

She lay, waiting for the fire to leave her legs, shaking so hard that her lamp beam danced. Then she got to her knees, braced herself and gave three hard tugs on the line.

A few minutes later, Barry emerged and collapsed beside her, his eyes still full of the horror of the journey. He reached out a shaking hand and clasped her wrist. 'How you did that without even knowing there was a way through, I'll never know –'

'It seemed like hours.'

Barry nodded. 'You were only a few minutes,

really, but the water's rising at a fair rate. It was up to the third step when I left.'

One by one, the others dragged themselves from the cross-cut. Mr Pugh was the last. Mark Daniels had to go back in and help him out. He kneeled just beside the cross-cut, fighting for air. Inching through it seemed to have taken up all his strength and self-control and his face hung below the helmet lamp like a Hallowe'en mask. Barry and Mark slung his arms over their shoulders, pulled him to his feet and on they went.

It was the hint of rain and grass in the air that brought Ruth to a halt. Debbie stopped beside her and took a deep breath. 'I can smell –'

'– fresh air,' finished Ruth. She took a few steps forward and stared into the darkness. 'Look,' she breathed, pointing to the pale smudge of grey. 'It's the shaft!'

They ran. Barry and Mark brought up the rear, half-dragging Mr Pugh between them. The darkness hid potholes and piles of rubble and projecting elbows of granite, but still they ran. They could not help it. The smudge grew into a square and the air paled around them. Carol Yelland was well out in front when the ground creaked and gave way beneath her. She screamed and stumbled backwards until she reached solid rock again, then stood, staring wide-eyed at the rotting planks of wood that lay between her and the light.

They were faced with a bridge of sorts, put in by the miners after the tunnel floor had collapsed into the level below. Two thick lengths of timber had been set across the gap and planks of wood had been chained to them like the rungs of a ladder. Then more planks had been piled lengthwise over the top to make a rough road. The whole mass was rotting and rusting away.

Ruth stared at the bridge, her eyes sparking with anger. Oh no, you don't, she thought. You're not going to have them. I won't let you.

'Right,' she snapped, whirling to face the others. 'Into a line over here. Hurry! Now, Barry, you rope everyone together. Plenty of space between each one. And I want at least four yards of line left at the front.'

Barry hesitated, glancing at Mr Pugh who was clinging to Mark Daniels and desperately sucking air into his lungs.

'Come on!' yelled Ruth. 'He's out of it. He's not going to tell us what to do.'

Barry moved quickly down the line, tying the knots he had learned on his father's fishing boat. As he worked, Ruth talked.

'OK. See this thick timber running right the way along? That's where we're going to cross.'

'Hang on a minute,' said Barry. 'What about him?' He jerked a thumb at Mr Pugh. 'He can't balance across there. Look at the state of him.'

'Leave him,' muttered Debbie, glancing nervously back down the level. 'We can go and get help.'

'We can't leave him here,' said Carol flatly. 'That door could go any minute. We'll have to carry him across somehow.'

'But he's a man,' whined Debbie, 'and we're only kids –'

'Come off it,' said Mark. 'Carol's bigger than he is. He can't weigh that much.'

'I've got it,' said Barry. 'If I can truss him up so he's

175

swinging from the rope in a sort of hammock, me and Mark can carry him across between us.'

'Just do it!' shouted Debbie. 'And let's get out of here.'

Minutes later, Barry and Mark stood roped together at the end of the line and Mr Pugh lay between them, tied to the rope at chest, waist and knees.

'Ready?' asked Barry, glancing over his shoulder. Mark nodded. 'OK. Now we kneel down. Put the line over your shoulder, like this, and . . . up!'

They staggered to their feet. Mr Pugh's head flopped back. His eyes rolled open and he began to flail his arms around.

'Keep still, sir!' yelled Mark. 'We've got you. Get hold of the rope above your head.'

At the sound of Mark's voice, Mr Pugh stopped thrashing around. He raised his head and, with a great effort, wrapped his arms around the line.

'Good,' said Ruth. 'I'll cross first. Nobody follows until I've wrapped the rope around that spur of rock in the wall there. That way you're anchored if the timber breaks or someone slips.'

'And if you slip?' asked Debbie.

'Just watch me,' said Ruth, picking up the end of the line.

'Tie it round your waist –' began Carol, but Ruth was already moving.

She almost flew across, never letting her weight settle. Rusty lengths of chain grated and clinked, planks of wood splintered and went clattering down into the darkness, but the main support held.

'Easy!' she called. 'Just keep moving. Ready? Go!'

They shuttled across like beads on an abacus. The

ones who might have hesitated had no choice but to go as the rope tightened in front of them. Barry and Mark brought up the rear with Mr Pugh dangling between them.

Barry had just reached safety when the beam gave a loud crack and sagged in the middle. The beam end ahead of Mark rose slowly from the ground and began to slip down over the edge. Mark lifted one large foot, planted it on the sliding beam end and boosted himself up on to solid rock as the bridge collapsed behind him. He made it look as simple as stepping from an escalator.

They gave a ragged cheer as they headed for the opening of the shaft, still roped together. 'Yes!' cried Ruth. 'We're here!'

She began to climb, fighting her way up the pile of loose rubble blocking the tunnel. A boulder shifted under her foot and she fell back, grabbing at a spar of wood that crumbled into dust. A piece of rusty metal tore into her calf but she kept going and the others climbed with her.

Above the rubble, the shaft angled gently to the sky and the granite gave enough holds for them to climb hand over hand, avoiding the rotting ladders. They were halfway to the top when a dull boom reverberated from below.

'The door –'

'Climb! Climb!'

Torn fingers, a shower of stones, trampling feet. But the water was faster. It surged through the passages and boiled up the shaft towards them. Mr Pugh was sucked down first. His arm came up once in an almost casual wave. Mark Daniels fought frantically to stay above water but the smooth strength of the undercurrents swallowed him down too.

The whole chain began to falter and slide, like a human avalanche. 'Dig in!' screamed Ruth, grabbing the rope and leaning back against it so hard, she felt her muscles tear. They clung to the wet shaft side with aching fingers and held . . . and held . . . And the water fell back, drawn to its natural level.

Mark and Mr Pugh were left hanging from the rope, soaking wet and coughing up sea water.

'Good knots, those,' said Barry, with pride.

They found a new cliff edge at the top of the shaft. The engine house was gone and the air smelt of newly exposed earth. They scrambled to safety and came to a halt in the wind and the rain; soaked, bloodied and trembling with exhaustion. Mark hauled Mr Pugh up the last few feet and laid him tenderly on the grass. Barry began to untie knots and they winced as the rope burns started to hurt, but nobody spoke. They breathed the fresh air and looked up at the sky.

When the man came puffing over the rise from the valley below, bristling with climbing gear, they stared at him as though he had arrived from another world. He stared back, then turned and shouted down the valley, 'They're here!'

Within minutes the clifftop was full of rescuers. They were checked for injuries and wrapped in foil insulating blankets like chickens. Radios squawked and crackled. A helicopter blatt-blatted overhead.

'Any still down there?' shouted one man, bending over Mr Pugh.

'No one.'

'So you lost only one?'

178

'No one,' repeated Mr Pugh, struggling to sit up. 'We lost no one.'

The man looked puzzled. 'But we brought one out of the tramming level. Found him lying at the edge of the rock fall. 'He'd been hit by a ruddy great chunk of granite.'

'Ben . . .' croaked Ruth, staggering to the top of the rise. Down below an ambulance waited, blue light flashing, and two men were carrying a stretcher up the valley. A red blanket covered him but she could just see the top of his dark head. He was still.

'Ben!'

The man came up and put his arm around her shoulders. 'Now come on, calm down, love. He can't hear you. He's out cold. They had to give him a shot to get his dislocated shoulder back in place.'

'Dis– dislocated shoulder? Is that all?'

'And a nasty bump on the head. They're taking him in overnight for observation.'

'A nasty –' Ruth reached up, grabbed the man by his ears and planted a kiss on the end of his nose.

'It's a nasty bump on the head!' she sang, punching the air. Then she turned and ran down the hillside towards the stretcher, whooping and sliding all the way.

Other great reads ~~from~~ **Red Fox**

Further Red Fox titles that you might enjoy reading are listed on the following pages. They are available in bookshops or they can be ordered directly from us.

If you would like to order books, please send this form and the money due to:

ARROW BOOKS, BOOKSERVICE BY POST, PO BOX 29, DOUGLAS, ISLE OF MAN, BRITISH ISLES. Please enclose a cheque or postal order made out to Arrow Books Ltd for the amount due, plus 30p per book for postage and packing to a maximum of £3.00, both for orders within the UK. For customers outside the UK, please allow 35p per book.

NAME _____

ADDRESS _____

_____

Please print clearly.

Whilst every effort is made to keep prices low, it is sometimes necessary to increase cover prices at short notice. If you are ordering books by post, to save delay it is advisable to phone to confirm the correct price. The number to ring is THE SALES DEPARTMENT 071 (if outside London) 973 9700.

Other great reads ~ from **Red Fox**

Leap into humour and adventure with Joan Aiken

Joan Aiken writes wild adventure stories laced with comedy and melodrama that have made her one of the best-known writers today. Her James III series, which begins with *The Wolves of Willoughby Chase*, has been recognized as a modern classic. Packed with action from beginning to end, her books are a wild romp through a history that never happened.

THE WOLVES OF WILLOUGHBY CHASE

Even the wolves are not more evil than the cruel Miss Slighcarp . . .

ISBN 0 09 997250 6   £2.99

BLACK HEARTS IN BATTERSEA

Dr Field invited Simon to London – so why can't Simon find him?

ISBN 0 09 988860 2   £3.50

THE CUCKOO TREE

Deadly danger for Dido as she comes up against black magic.

ISBN 0 09 988870 X   £3.50

DIDO AND PA

Why is there a man with a bandaged face hiding in the attic?

ISBN 0 09 988850 5   £3.50

MIDNIGHT IS A PLACE

Thrown out of his home, Lucas must find a way to live in the cruel town of Blastburn.

ISBN 0 09 979200 1   £3.50

Other great reads from **Red Fox**

Enter the magical world of Dr Dolittle

Dr Dolittle is one of the great book characters – everyone knows the kindly doctor who can talk to the animals. With his household of animals – Too-Too the owl, Dab-Dab the duck, Gub-gub the pig and Jip the dog – and Tommy Stubbins, his assistant, he finds himself in and out of trouble, of money and of England in a series of adventures. These editions have been sensitively edited with the approval of Christopher Lofting, the author's son.

THE STORY OF DOCTOR DOLITTLE
ISBN 0 09 985470 8 £3.99

THE VOYAGES OF DOCTOR DOLITTLE
ISBN 0 09 985470 8 £4.99

DR DOLITTLE'S POST OFFICE
ISBN 0 09 988040 7 £4.99

DR DOLITTLE'S CIRCUS
ISBN 0 09 985440 6 £4.99

DR DOLITTLE'S ZOO
ISBN 0 09 988030 X £4.99

DR DOLITTLE'S GARDEN
ISBN 0 09 988050 4 £4.99

DR DOLITTLE IN THE MOON
ISBN 0 09 988060 1 £4.99

DR DOLITTLE'S CARAVAN
ISBN 0 09 985450 3 £4.99

DR DOLITTLE AND THE GREEN CANARY
ISBN 0 09 988090 3 £4.99

Other great reads *from* **Red Fox**

Paul Zindel – the king of young adult fiction

Sad, but comic and seriously off-the-wall, Paul Zindel's books for young adults are unputdownable.

A STAR FOR THE LATECOMER
with Bonnie Zindel

Brooke's mother would give anything for Brooke to be a star – but her mother's dying.

ISBN 0 09 987200 5   £2.99

A BEGONIA FOR MISS APPLEBAUM

'Miss Applebaum was the most special teacher we ever had . . .'

ISBN 0 09 987210 2   £2.99

THE GIRL WHO WANTED A BOY

Sybella knows more about carburettors than boys – but she wants one, badly.

ISBN 0 09 987180 7   £2.99

THE UNDERTAKER'S GONE BANANAS

No one will believe him but Bobby knows he saw the undertaker strangling his wife.

ISBN 0 09 987190 4   £2.99

Other great reads ✦ *from* **Red Fox**

Discover the Red Fox poetry collections

CADBURY'S NINTH BOOK OF CHILDREN'S POETRY

Poems by children aged 4–16.

ISBN 0 09 983450 2   £4.99

THE COMPLETE SCHOOL VERSE
ed. Jennifer Curry

Two books in one all about school.

ISBN 0 09 991790 4   £2.99

MY NAME, MY POEM ed. Jennifer Curry

Find *your* name in this book.

ISBN 0 09 948030 1   £1.95

MONSTROSITIES Charles Fuge

Grim, gruesome poems about monsters.

ISBN 0 09 967330 4   £3.50

LOVE SHOUTS AND WHISPERS Vernon Scannell

Read about all sorts of love in this book.

ISBN 0 09 973950 X   £2.99

CATERPILLAR STEW Gavin Ewart

A collection describing all sorts of unusual animals.

ISBN 0 09 967280 4   £2.50

HYSTERICALLY HISTORICAL Gordon Snell and Wendy Shea

Madcap rhymes from olden times

ISBN 0 09 972160 0   £2.99

Other great reads from **Red Fox**

Spinechilling stories to read at night

THE CONJUROR'S GAME Catherine Fisher

Alick has unwittingly set something unworldly afoot in Halcombe Great Wood.

ISBN 0 09 985960 2   £2.50

RAVENSGILL William Mayne

What is the dark secret that has held two families apart for so many years?

ISBN 0 09 975270 0   £2.99

EARTHFASTS William Mayne

The bizarre chain of events begins when David and Keith see someone march out of the ground . . .

ISBN 0 09 977600 6   £2.99

A LEGACY OF GHOSTS Colin Dann

Two boys go searching for old Mackie's hoard and find something else . . .

ISBN 0 09 986540 8   £2.99

TUNNEL TERROR

The Channel Tunnel is under threat and only Tom can save it . . .

ISBN 0 09 989030 5   £2.99

Other great reads from **Red Fox**

Superb historical stories from Rosemary Sutcliff

Rosemary Sutcliff tells the historical story better than anyone else. Her tales are of times filled with high adventure, desperate enterprises, bloody encounters and tender romance. Discover the vividly real world of Rosemary Sutcliff today!

THE CAPRICORN BRACELET
ISBN 0 09 977620 0   £2.50

KNIGHT'S FEE
ISBN 0 09 977630 8   £2.99

THE SHINING COMPANY
ISBN 0 09 985580 1   £3.50

THE WITCH'S BRAT
ISBN 0 09 975080 5   £2.50

SUN HORSE, MOON HORSE
ISBN 0 09 979550 7   £2.50

TRISTAN AND ISEULT
ISBN 0 09 979550 7   £2.99

BEOWULF: DRAGON SLAYER
ISBN 0 09 997270 0   £2.50

THE HOUND OF ULSTER
ISBN 0 09 997260 3   £2.99

THE LIGHT BEYOND THE FOREST
ISBN 0 09 997450 9   £2.99

THE SWORD AND THE CIRCLE
ISBN 0 09 997460 6   £2.99